To Aunt Pa
& Uncle

It's a nice
surprise to see you!

Love-
Kathy

1-20-97

The Yearbook of Hope and Inspiration

Go, little book, and wish to all
Flowers in the garden, meat in the hall,
A bin of wine, a spice of wit,
A house with lawns enclosing it,
A living river by the door,
A nightingale in the sycamore!

Robert Louis Stevenson

Also by Celia Haddon
published by Michael Joseph

A BOOK OF FRIENDS AND FRIENDSHIP

A CHRISTMAS POSY

A LOVER'S POSY

A MOTHER'S POSY

THE POWERS OF LOVE

GIFTS FROM YOUR GARDEN

CELIA HADDON

The Yearbook of Hope and Inspiration

MICHAEL JOSEPH

LONDON

To
Peggy Challis

MICHAEL JOSEPH LTD
Published by the Penguin Group
27 Wrights Lane, London W8 5TZ, England
Viking Penguin Inc., 40 West 23rd Street, New York, New York, 10010 USA
Penguin Books Canada Ltd. 2801 John Street, Markham Ontario, Canada L3R 1B4
Penguin Books (NZ). 182-190 Wairau Road, Auckland 10, New Zealand

Penguin Books Ltd. Registered Offices Harmondsworth, Middlesex, England

First published in Great Britain October 1989
Second impression June 1990

Designed by Penny Mills
Printed and bound in Italy by Olivotto

A CIP catalogue record for this book is available from the British Library

ISBN 0 7181 3217 3

Library of Congress Catalog Card Number: 90-60566

For years friends have been giving me useful quotations and inspiring passages. I have written them in the front of my diary, put them onto a special file in my word processor, pinned them up above my desk or carried them around in my handbag reading them till the paper was almost illegible.

In the day to day struggle to live happily, I have often turned to these quotations for help. They have given me moments of insight into the human heart, reminders of the beauty of the world around me, or help in leading my life when inner peace seemed out of reach. Now in *The Book of Hope and Inspiration*, I want to share some of the quotations and sayings that have helped me.

The book is illustrated by paintings some of which were painted by my mother, the painter Joyce Haddon, a member of the New English Art Club and the Royal Society of British Artists. Other illustrations come from my own collection of Victorian children's books and early Christmas cards – a passionate hobby.

JANUARY

JANUARY 1

The American psychologist and philosopher William James had wise things to say about resolutions, often taken at New Year. In the acquisition of a new habit, or the leaving off of an old one, we must take care to launch ourselves with as strong and decided an initiative as possible . . . Never suffer an exception to occur till the new habit is securely rooted in your life. Each lapse is like the letting fall of a ball of string which one is carefully winding up: a single slip undoes more than a great many turns will wind again.

JANUARY 2

If you love, you will be loved;
If you respect people, you will be respected;
If you serve them, you will be served;
If you give a good account of yourself toward others,
    others will act likewise toward you.
Blessed is the man who loves and does not desire to
    be loved for it;
Blessed is he who respects others and does not look
    for respect in return;
Who serves and does not expect service for it; who
    acquits himself well of others and does not desire
    that they return the grace.
Because such things are big, foolish people do not rise
    to them.

BROTHER GILES

JANUARY 3   Courage is resistance to
fear, mastery of fear,
not absence of fear.

MARK TWAIN

JANUARY 4   *The Value of a Smile is a
piece of prose which first
appeared as an advertisement.
As I read it, I always end
up smiling to myself. Try for yourself.*

It costs nothing, but creates much.

It enriches those who receive, without impoverishing
those who give.

It happens in a flash, and the memory of it sometimes
lasts for ever.

None are so rich they can get along without it, and
none so poor but are richer for its benefits.

It creates happiness in the home, fosters good will in
a business, and is the countersign of friends.

It is rest to the weary, daylight to the discouraged, sunshine to
the sad, and Nature's best antidote for trouble.

Yet it cannot be bought, begged, borrowed or stolen,
for it is something that is no earthly good to anybody
till it is given away!

JANUARY

The world is new each morning – that is God's gift, and a man should believe he is reborn each day.

JANUARY 5

ISRAEL BEN ELIEZER

Today is the twelfth day of Christmas, the day of the epiphany, of which G.K. Chesterton wrote

JANUARY 6

There were three things prefigured and promised by the gifts in Bethlehem concerning the Child who received them; that He should be crowned like a king: that He should be worshipped like a God; and that He should die like a man. And these things would sound like Eastern flattery, were it not for the third.

Give up money, give up fame, give up science, give up the earth itself and all it contains, rather than do an immoral act.

JANUARY 7

THOMAS JEFFERSON

In hope a king doth go to war;
In hope a lover lives full long;
In hope a merchant sails full far;
In hope just men do suffer wrong;
In hope the ploughman sows his seed:
Thus hope helps thousands at their need.
Then faint not, heart, among the rest;
Whatever chance, hope thou the best.

JANUARY 8

ANONYMOUS

JANUARY 9   *The seventeenth-century mystic Thomas Traherne writes about human love in a beautiful way.*

You are as prone to love as the sun is to shine, it being the most delightful and natural employment of the soul of man, without which you are dark and miserable. Consider therefore the extent of love, its vigour and excellency. For certainly he that delights not in love makes vain the universe, and is of necessity to himself the greatest burden.

JANUARY 10   In much of your talking, thinking is half murdered.
For thought is a bird of space, that in a cage of words may indeed unfold its wings but cannot fly.

KAHLIL GIBRAN

JANUARY 11   Earth's common pleasures, near the ground like grass,
Are best of all; nor die although they fade:
Dear, simple household joys, that straightway pass
The precinct of devotion, undismayed.

WILLIAM ALLINGHAM

JANUARY 12   *It is about now that some of my New Year resolutions falter and this prayer helps me.* O Lord God, when Thou givest to Thy servants to endeavour any great matter, grant us also to know that it is not the beginning, but the continuing of the same, until it be thoroughly finished, which yieldeth the true glory.

There is a wisdom which isn't found in books or from learned experts. JANUARY 13
We will find it in the human hearts of the people around us. The
essayist William Hazlitt described it this way: You will hear more
good things on the outside of a stage-coach from London to
Oxford than if you were to pass a twelvemonth with the
undergraduates, or heads of colleges, of that famous univer-
sity; and more home truths are to be learnt from listening to a
noisy debate in an alehouse than from attending a formal one
in the House of Commons.

Creating something, whether it is a painting or a piece of embroidery, JANUARY 14
some music or perhaps just making a magnificent snowman, brings one
closer to the divine. It is the making, rather than the results, that brings
joy us the poet Robert Bridges points out.

> I too will something make
> And joy in the making;
> Altho' tomorrow it seem
> Like the empty words of a dream
> Remembered on waking.

JANUARY 15   *In mid January the cold weather often transforms the world with frost or snow. The country poet John Clare describes the beauty that it brings.*

> Winter is come in earnest and the snow
> In dazzling splendour – crumping underfoot –
> Spreads a white world all calm, and where we go
> By hedge or wood, trees shine from top to root
> In feathered foliage flashing light and shade
> Of strangest contrast. Fancy's pliant eye
> Delighted sees a vast romance displayed
> And fairy halls descended from the sky.

JANUARY 16   *Kitty Muggeridge tells this story about a wealthy merchant who was in despair.* He wondered why. He asked his companions how he could find happiness. 'Look for a happy man,' they told him, 'and ask him to give you his shirt.' The merchant searched for a long time until at last he found a happy man. 'Give me your shirt,' he said. 'I can pay for it.' The happy man began to laugh uproariously; he hadn't got a shirt! Then the merchant understood the cause of his own despair: man cannot live by bread alone.

The Lord's Prayer contains 56 words, the Ten Command-
ments 297, the American Declaration of Independence 300.
The European Economic Community Directive on the Export
of Duck Eggs contains 26,911 words, *reported the Sunday
Express in 1977. It's a relief to remember that the most important
things don't always take up the most words!*

Why restless, why cast down, my soul?
Hope still, and thou shalt sing
The praise of Him who is thy God
Thy health's eternal spring.

NAHUM TATE

Trust the past to God's mercy, the present to His love, and the
future to His providence.

ST AUGUSTINE

On the wind of January
Down flits the snow,
Travelling from the frozen North
As cold as it can blow.
Poor robin redbreast,
Look where he comes;
Let him in to feel your fire
And toss him of your crumbs.

CHRISTINA ROSSETTI

JANUARY 21   *Now is the time for warm fires. The witty writer Sydney Smith knew the value of a fire.* Never neglect your fireplaces: I have paid great attention to mine. Much of the cheerfulness of life depends upon it. Who could be miserable with that fire? What makes a fire so pleasant is that it is a live thing in a dead room.

JANUARY 22

Nature, as far as in her lies,
Imitates God and turns her face
To every land beneath the skies,
Counts nothing that she meets with base
But lives and loves in every place.

ALFRED LORD TENNYSON

JANUARY 23   How ridiculous it would be to see the sheep endeavouring to walk like the dog, or the ox striving to trot like the horse; just as ridiculous it is to see one man striving to imitate another. Man varies from man more than animal from animal of different species, *wrote William Blake. Comparing ourselves with others leads us to envy others or to feel failures.*

JANUARY 24

Think not thy wisdom can illume away
The ancient tanglement of night and day.
Enough, to acknowledge both, and both revere:
They see not clearliest who see all things clear.

We need acceptance not wisdom, says William Watson.

Some haw meat, and canna eat,
And some wad eat that want it;
But we hae meat and we can eat,
And sae the Lord be thankit.

Today is Burns Night. This simple grace for meal times was written by Robert Burns, the greatest of Scottish poets whose memory is kept alive all over the world on this particular day of the year. It reminds me to be grateful for my daily bread.

We ourselves feel that what we are doing is just a drop in the ocean. But if that drop was not in the ocean, I think the ocean would be less because of that missing drop. I do not agree with the big way of doing things. To us what matters is an individual. To get to love the person we must come in close contact with him. If we wait till we get the numbers, then we will be lost in the numbers. *Mother Teresa of Calcutta has devoted her whole life to helping the destitute in India yet here she is saying that we can all do our bit to help – even if what we can do is only a little.*

JANUARY 27   *The key to living through pain and unhappiness is just acceptance. These words by the theologian Paul Tillich have comforted me when I am depressed.* Grace strikes us when we are in great pain and restlessness. It strikes us when we walk through the dark valley of a meaningless and empty life. It strikes us when our disgust for our own being, our indifference, our weakness, our hostility, and our lack of direction and composure have become intolerable to us. It strikes us when, year after year, the longed-for perfection of life does not appear, when the old compulsions reign within us as they have for decades, when despair destroys all joy and courage. Sometimes at that moment a wave of light breaks into our darkness, and it is as though a voice were saying: 'You are accepted.'

JANUARY 28

        Is it so small a thing
        To have enjoyed the sun,
        To have lived light in the spring,
        To have loved, to have thought, to have done?

It's not a small thing at all, of course. But it takes this verse by Matthew Arnold to remind me.

Bishop Thomas Wilson wrote down this recipe for happiness two hundred years ago. It's still true.

Happy life. Lay nothing much to heart; desire nothing too eagerly; rejoice not excessively, nor grieve too much for disasters; be not bent violently on any design; and above all, let no worldly cares make you forget the concerns of your soul.

All experience is an arch wherethro'
Gleams that untravelled world, whose margins fade
For ever and for ever when I move.

These lines of Alfred Tennyson's describe the spiritual life we lead, sometimes unaware it is there.

One simple mental trick has changed my life. A wise retired railway worker called Danny Breslin told me about it. When you are faced with a task you do not want to perform, do not think of the task as a whole. Do not focus on the hardest part of it. Instead, ask yourself: 'What is the least I can do towards this task? What is the irreducible minimum?' Do that and you have started on the task itself. So, for instance, if you are procrastinating about a letter you have to write, put aside the thought of the letter itself and what you will say in it. Instead, think of the least thing you can do towards it, which is getting a pen and paper ready. By doing this you will usually find that you can then actually start writing the letter itself.

FEBRUARY

Have HOPE! though clouds environ round,
And gladness hides her face in scorn,
Put thou the shadow from thy brow –
No night but has its morn.

Have FAITH! where'er thy bark is driven –
The calm's disport, the tempest's mirth –
Know this: God rules the hosts of heaven,
The inhabitants of earth.

Have LOVE! Not love alone for one,
But man as man thy brother call,
And scatter, like the circling sun,
Thy charities on all.

I love this poem by the German poet Friedrich Schiller.

Today is the medieval feast of Candlemas, when candles were lit in
parish churches for the Virgin Mary – a lovely custom. Real fire,
whether it's candlelight or the log fire puts a special glow into a room.
Percy Bysshe Shelley wrote about its beauty.

Men scarcely know how beautiful fire is –
Each flame of it is as a precious stone
Dissolved in ever-moving light, and this
Belongs to each and all who gaze upon.

FEBRUARY 3

Stay, stay at home, my heart, and rest;
Home-keeping hearts are happiest,
For those that wander they know not where
Are full of trouble and full of care;
To stay at home is best!

Weary and homesick and distressed
They wander east, they wander west,
And are baffled and beaten and blown about
By the winds of the wilderness of doubt;
To stay at home is best.

Then stay at home, my heart, and rest;
The bird is safest in its nest;
O'er all that flutter their wings and fly
A hawk is hovering in the sky;
To stay at home is best.

HENRY WADSWORTH LONGFELLOW

Beauty is God's handwriting. Welcome it in every fair face, every fair day, every fair flower.

FEBRUARY 4

CHARLES KINGSLEY

There's a lovely Jewish story about a holy Rabbi which says a lot about the real spirit of charity to others.

FEBRUARY 5

'Go, give a penny to that blind beggar,' said the Rabbi of Witkowo to his son, when they were walking together. The boy did so. When he rejoined his father, 'Why didst thou not raise thy hat?' asked the Rabbi. 'But he is blind,' replied the boy. 'He could not have seen me.' 'And how dost thou know,' retorted his father, 'that he is not an impostor. Go, raise thy hat.'

Why are thou cast down, O my soul? and why art thou disquieted in me? hope thou in God: for I shall yet
    praise him for the help of his countenance.
O my God, my soul is cast down within me: therefore
will I remember thee from the land of Jordan, and of
    the Hermonites, from the hill Mizar.
Deep calleth to deep at the noise of thy waterspouts:
    all thy waves and thy billows are gone over me.
Yet the Lord will command his loving kindness in the
daytime, and in the night his song shall be with me,
    and my prayer unto the God of my life.

FEBRUARY 6

PSALM 42

'Don't you worry and don't you hurry.' I know that phrase by heart, and if all the other music should perish out of the world it would still sing to me.

FEBRUARY 7

MARK TWAIN

FEBRUARY 8 We have a call to do good, as often as we have the power and the occasion.

WILLIAM PENN

FEBRUARY 9 *Two hundred years ago, this little verse was hung up in schools to remind children to be kind to animals.*

> A man of kindness to his beast is kind,
> But brutal actions show a brutal mind.
> Remember, He who made thee, made the brute;
> Who gave thee speech and reason, formed him mute.
> He can't complain, but God's all-seeing eye
> Beholds thy cruelty – He hears his cry.

FEBRUARY 10 Divers men may walk by the sea side, and the same beams of the sun giving light to them all, one gathereth by the benefit of that light pebbles or speckled shells for curious vanity, and another gathers precious pearl or medicinal amber by the same light.

This is a lovely way to say that life is what we make of it. It comes from a sermon by the poet John Donne.

FEBRUARY 11
> The trivial round, the common task
> Would furnish all we ought to ask, –
> Room to deny ourselves, a road
> To bring us daily nearer God.

JOHN KEBLE

FEBRUARY

A friend of mine Guy Louis Decanonville said something so wise that I've remembered it for years.

You cannot be like someone else. You have to shine by your own light: you cannot shine with another's light.

Slow me down, Lord!
Ease the pounding of my heart by the quieting of my mind.
Steady my hurried pace with a vision of the eternal reach of
 time.
Give me, amid the confusion of the day, the calmness of the
 everlasting rills.
Break the tensions of my nerves and muscles with the
soothing music of the singing streams that live in my memory.
Help me to know the magical, restoring power of sleep.
Teach me the art of taking minute vacations – of slowing
down to look at a flower, to chat with a friend, to pat a dog, to
 read a few lines from a good book.

ORIN L. CRAIN

FEBRUARY 14

Love is not love
That alters when it alteration finds
Or bends with the remover to remove:
Oh no! It is an ever fixed mark
That looks on tempests and is never shaken;
It is the star to every wandering bark
Whose worth's unknown, although his height be taken.
Love's not Time's fool, though rosy lips and cheeks
Within his bending sickle's compass come;
Love alters not with his brief hours and weeks
But bears it out even to the edge of doom.

WILLIAM SHAKESPEARE

FEBRUARY 15

If I had to live my life again, I would have made a rule to read some poetry and listen to some music at least once every week; for perhaps the parts of my brain now atrophied would thus have been kept active through use. The loss of these tastes is a loss of happiness, and may possibly be injurious to the intellect, and more probably to the moral character.

A great scientist like Charles Darwin came to see that poetry and music are part of a balanced life.

FEBRUARY

But to love is better than to be loved. For love is an active
pleasure and a good thing; whilst merely to be loved creates
no activity in the soul. He that loves, in so far as he loves, is
conferring benefit; whilst he who is loved, in so far as he is
loved, confers none.

ARISTOTLE

We have to learn to cope with the anger of others, and to recognise our
own anger too. I find these verses by Robert Southwell, a seventeenth
century Catholic priest, helpful. He uses the old-fashioned word
'enlarged' where we would say 'enraged'.

> I wrestle not with rage,
> While fury's flame doth burn;
> It is in vain to stop the streams
> Until the tide doth turn.
>
> But when the flame is out,
> And ebbing wrath doth end,
> I turn a late enlarged foe
> Into a quiet friend.

There is a principle which is a bar against all information,
which is proof against all arguments and which cannot fail to
keep a man in everlasting ignorance – that principle is
contempt prior to investigation.

HERBERT SPENCER

FEBRUARY

FEBRUARY 19   Make books your compansions; let your bookshelves be your gardens: bask in their beauty, gather their fruit, pluck their roses, take their spices and myrrh.

IBN TIBBON

FEBRUARY 20   The time of frost is the time for me!
When the gay blood spins through the heart with glee
When the voice leaps out with a chiming sound,
And the footstep rings on the musical ground;
When earth is white, and air is bright,
And every breath a new delight!

And morning! – each pane a garden of frost,
Of delicate flowering, as quickly lost;
For the stalks are fed by the moon's cold beams,
And the leaves are woven like woof of dreams
By night's keen breath, and a glance of the sun
Like dreams will scatter them every one.

WILLIAM ALLINGHAM

FEBRUARY 21   Do what you can – and the task will rest lightly in your hand, so lightly that you will be able to look forward to the more difficult tests which may be awaiting you.

This thought comes from the notebook kept by Dag Hammarskjold, the United Nations Secretary General. Next time you're faced with a daunting task just remember all you have to do is 'Do what you can'.

Snowdrops are the first hopeful signs of spring's coming, described in a poem by William Wordsworth.

Lone flower, hemmed in with snows, and white as they
But hardier far, once more I see thee bend
Thy forehead as if fearful to offend,
Like an unbidden guest. Though day by day
Storms, sallying from the mountain tops, waylay
The rising sun, and on the plains descend;
Yet art thou welcome, welcome as a friend
Whose zeal outruns his promise! Blue-eyed May
Shall soon behold this border thickly set
With bright jonquils, their odours lavishing
On the soft west wind and his frolic peers;
Nor will I then thy modest grace forget,
Chaste snowdrop, venturous harbinger of spring,
And pensive monitor of fleeting years!

All God's life opens into the individual particular, and here and now, or nowhere, is reality. The present hour is the decisive hour and every day is doomsday.

RALPH WALDO EMERSON

FEBRUARY 24   *One of my favourite poets is the Dorset poet, William Barnes, who wrote in a West country dialect the poem, Linden Lea. Most people know its English version sung as a song: few know the original. But here is its last verse, about the pleasure of living in the country rather than making money in the town. If you say it out loud, the dialect is easier understood.*

> Let other volk make money vaster
> In the air o' dark-room'd towns,
> I don't dread a peevish master;
> Though noo man do heed my frowns,
> I be free to goo abroade,
> Or take again my homeward road
> To where, vor me, the apple tree
> Do lean down low in Linden Lea.

FEBRUARY 25   *It may seem odd to find a useful quotation out of a nonsense book like Alice in Wonderland by Lewis Carroll, but I have. I need to remember it daily!*

'If everybody minded their own business,' the Duchess said in a hoarse growl, 'the world would go round a deal faster than it does.'

FEBRUARY

Every valley drinks,
Every dell and hollow:
Where the kind rain sinks and sinks,
Green of spring will follow.

Yet a lapse of weeks
Buds will burst their edges,
Strip the wool-coats, glue-coats, streaks,
In the woods and hedges.

CHRISTINA ROSSETTI

FEBRUARY 26

Heaven is much more pleased to view a repentant sinner, than ninety-nine persons who have supported a course of undeviating rectitude. For that single effort by which we stop short in the downhill path to perdition, is itself a greater exertion of virtue than an hundred acts of justice, *wrote Oliver Goldsmith.*

FEBRUARY 27

The world is so full of a number of things,
I'm sure we should all be as happy as kings.

ROBERT LOUIS STEVENSON

FEBRUARY 28

Sweet February Twenty Nine! –
This is our grace-year, as I live!
Quick, now! this foolish heart of mine:
Seize thy prerogative!

WALTER DE LA MARE

FEBRUARY 29

MARCH

It is the first mild day of March:
Each minute sweeter than before,
The redbreast sings from the tall larch
That stands beside our door.

There is a blessing in the air,
Which seems a sense of joy to yield
To the bare trees, and mountains bare,
And grass in the green field.

Love, now a universal birth,
From heart to heart is stealing,
From earth to man, from man to earth:
– It is the hour of feeling.

This poem was written by William Wordsworth for his sister Dorothy, who encouraged and looked after him.

Almost all the great philosophies and religions agree that each human being should try to acquire unsparing self knowledge. More than a thousand years ago the Islamic teacher, Azid ibn Muhammad al-Nasafi, told this story about Mohammad's son-in-law, Ali.

When Ali asked Mohammad, 'What am I to do that I may not waste my time,' the Prophet answered: 'Learn to know thyself.'

MARCH 3

Four ducks on a pond,
A grass bank beyond,
A blue sky of spring,
White clouds on the wing,
What a little thing
To remember for years –
To remember with tears!

There are moments when we notice the strange beauty of the world about us – the thought behind these lines by William Allingham, an Irish Victorian poet.

MARCH 4

Nowadays we know that the mind affects the body. But 400 years ago Francis Bacon, the great writer, knew it too. In an essay on the healthy life he advised: As for the passions and studies of the mind; avoid envy; anxious fears; anger fretting inwards; joys and exhilarations in excess; sadness not communicated. Entertain hopes; mirth rather than joy; variety of delights, rather than surfeit of them; wonder and admiration, and therefore novelties; studies that fill the mind with splendid and illustrious objects, as histories, fables, and contemplations of nature.

MARCH

Know all you can, love all you can, do all you can – that is the whole duty of men. Be friends, in the truest sense, each to the other. There is nothing in all the world like friendship. *These wise words come from Thomas Davidson, an American philanthropist.*

MARCH 5

Some have too much, yet still do crave;
I have little, and seek no more.
They are but poor though much they have,
And I am rich with little store.
They poor, I rich; they beg, I give;
They lack, I leave; they pine, I live.

SIR EDWARD DYER

MARCH 6

As I got older I became aware of the folly of this perpetual reaching after the future, and of drawing from tomorrow and from tomorrow only, a reason for the joyfulness of today. I learned, alas! when it was almost too late, to live in each moment as it passed over my head, believing that the sun as it is now rising is as good as it will ever be.

MARK RUTHERFORD

MARCH 7

Stoop where thou wilt, thy careless hand
Some random bud will meet;
Thou canst not tread, but thou wilt find
The daisy at thy feet.

A lovely spring song from the poet Thomas Hood.

MARCH 8

MARCH 9   The fact is, that in order to do anything in this world worth doing, we must not stand shivering on the bank, and thinking of the cold and the danger, but jump in and scramble through as well as we can. It will not do to be perpetually calculating risks, and adjusting nice chances. *The eighteenth-century writer Sydney Smith, a man of wit and sense, gave this good advice.*

MARCH 10

If I can stop one heart from breaking,
I shall not live in vain;
If I can ease one life the aching,
Or cool one pain,
Or help one fainting robin
Unto his nest again,
I shall not live in vain.

EMILY DICKINSON

MARCH 11   *This month flower sellers start selling early daffodils. A. A. Milne, best known for his children's books about Winnie-the-Pooh, obviously enjoyed those early yellow trumpets as much as I do.*

A house with daffodils in it is a house lit up, whether or no the sun be shining outside. Daffodils in a green bowl – and let it snow if it will.

MARCH 12

If I am like someone else who will be like me?

JEWISH SAYING

The great Indian classic book, The Geeta, tells the story of the god, **MARCH 13**
Krishna. He has this to say:

It is better to do one's own duty, however defective it may be, than to follow the duty of another, however well one may perform it. He who does his duty as his own nature reveals it, never sins.

Welcome, pale primrose! starting up between **MARCH 14**
Dead matted leaves of ash and oak that strew
The every lawn, the wood and spinney through,
'Mid creeping moss and ivy's darker green;
How much thy presence beautifies the ground!
How sweet thy modest unaffected pride
Glows on the sunny bank and wood's warm side.
And where thy fairy flowers in groups are found,
The schoolboy roams enchantedly along,
Plucking the fairest with a rude delight;
While the meek shepherd stops his simple song,
To gaze a moment on the pleasing sight;
O'erjoyed to see the flowers that truly bring
The welcome news of sweet returning spring.

JOHN CLARE

MARCH 15   *For all those who love animals, there is an inspiring story about the Celtic saint, St Kevin, which I found in a book called Beasts and Saints by Helen Waddell.*

At one Lenten season, St Kevin, as was his way, fled from the company of men to a certain solitude, and in a little hut that did but keep out the sun and the rain, gave himself earnestly to reading and to prayer, and his leisure to contemplation alone. And as he knelt in his accustomed fashion, with his hand outstretched through the window and lifted up to heaven, a blackbird settled on it and busying herself as in her nest, laid in it an egg. And so moved was the saint that in all patience and gentleness he remained, neither closing nor withdrawing his hand; but until the young ones were fully hatched he held it out unwearied, shaping it for the purpose.

MARCH 16
Happy the man, and happy he alone,
He who can call today his own:
He who, secure within, can say
Tomorrow do thy worst, for I have lived today.

JOHN DRYDEN

MARCH

MARCH 17

For St Patrick's Day this charming Irish blessing.

May you have food and raiment, a soft pillow for your head, and may you be half an hour in heaven before the Devil knows you're there.

MARCH 18

Self-love but serves the virtuous mind to wake,
As the small pebble stirs the peaceful lake;
The centre moved, a circle straight succeeds,
Another still and still another spreads;
Friend, parent, neighbour first it will embrace;
His country next; and next all human race.

ALEXANDER POPE

MARCH 19

Have courage for the great sorrows of life and patience for the small ones.

VICTOR HUGO

MARCH 20

One star
Is better far
Than many precious stones:
One sun, which is above in glory seen,
Is worth ten thousand golden thrones:
A juicy herb or spire of grass
In useful virtue, native green,
An emerald doth surpass,
Hath in't more value, though less seen.

THOMAS TRAHERNE

MARCH 21   A wise man will make haste to forgive, because he who knows the true value of time will not suffer it to pass away in unnecessary pain. He that willingly suffers the corrosions of inveterate hatred, and gives up his days and nights to the gloom of malice, cannot surely be said to consult his own ease. Resentment is the union of sorrow with malignity, a combination of a passion which all endeavour to avoid, with a passion which all concur to detest. *To be happy we need to forgive others, according to Dr Samuel Johnson.*

MARCH 22   The man that is open of heart to his neighbour,
And stops to consider his likes and dislikes,
His blood shall be wholesome whatever his labour,
His luck shall be with him whatever he strikes.

RUDYARD KIPLING

MARCH 23   Every blade of grass, each leaf, each separate floret and petal, is an inscription speaking of hope.

RICHARD JEFFRIES

MARCH 24   I'll act with prudence as far as I'm able;
But if success I must never find,
Then come misfortune, I bid thee welcome,
I'll meet thee with an undaunted mind.

Robert Burns used to repeat this verse to himself when faced with the many setbacks of his life.

The truth of the flower is, not the facts about it, but the shining, glowing, gladdening, patient thing throned on its stalk – the compeller of smile and tear ... The idea of God *is* the flower: His idea is not the botany of the flower. Its botany is but a thing of ways and means – of canvas and colour and brush in relation to the picture in the painter's brain.

MARCH 25

GEORGE MACDONALD

March is the month when we can often see lambs, gambolling about in the fields. Each spring the sight reminds me of this poem by William Blake.

MARCH 26

> Little lamb, who made thee?
> Dost thou know who made thee,
> Gave thee life, and bade thee feed
> By the stream and o'er the mead;
> Gave thee clothing of delight,
> Softest clothing, woolly, bright;
> Gave thee such a tender voice,
> Making all the vales rejoice?
> Little lamb, who made thee?
> Dost thou know who made thee?

MARCH 27 It seems to me that the whole secret of life, if it is to be happy, is in the spirit of love; and when an old form of love dies we must take on the new. If life is to be made interesting and worth its breath, we must look on ourselves as growing children, right up to the end of our days. So that when a man grows old on the pleasures of a city, and loses his appetite for them, he would be wise to renew his love of life in a garden that is green and quiet, and always full of interest. It must be remembered too that the greatest joy that comes from a garden is in doing the work ourselves; for things that are planted by our own hands have a special interest in their growth.

W. H. DAVIES

MARCH 28 *My favourite hymn was written by John Newman.*
Lead, kindly Light, amid the encircling gloom,
Lead Thou me on!
The night is dark and I am far from home –
Lead Thou me on!
Keep Thou my feet: I do not ask to see
The distant scene, – one step enough for me.

MARCH

To be loved, and to love, need courage, the courage to judge MARCH 29
certain values as of ultimate concern – and to take the jump
and stake everything on these values.

Erich Fromm

It is easy in the world to live after the world's opinion; it is MARCH 30
easy in solitude to live after our own; but the great man is he
who in the midst of the crowd keeps with perfect sweetness
the independence of solitude.

Ralph Waldo Emerson

Today – Mend a quarrel. Search out a forgotten friend. MARCH 31
Dismiss suspicion and replace it with trust. Write a love letter.
Share some treasure. Give a soft answer. Encourage youth.
Manifest your loyalty in a word or a deed.

Today – Keep a promise. Find the time. Forego a grudge.
Forgive an enemy. Listen. Apologize if you were wrong. Try
to understand. Flout envy. Examine your demands on others.
Think first of someone else. Appreciate, be kind, be gentle.
Laugh a little more.

Today – Deserve confidence. Take up arms against malice.
Decry complacency. Express your gratitude. Worship your
God. Gladden the heart of a child. Take pleasure in the beauty
and wonder of the earth. Speak it again. Speak it still again.
Speak it still once again.

Author unknown

APRIL

The first of April, some do say,
Is set apart for All Fools' Day,
But why the people call it so,
Nor I, nor they themselves do know.
But on this day are people sent
On purpose for pure merriment.
But 'tis a thing to be disputed,
Which is the greatest Fool reputed,
The Man that innocently went,
Or he that him designedly sent.

APRIL 1

POOR ROBIN'S ALMANACK FOR 1760

It is during this month, that those of us lucky enough to have a garden (or even just a windowbox) start planning for summer. I love these words by the seventeenth-century writer, Francis Bacon: God Almighty first planted a garden. And indeed it is one of the purest of human pleasures. It is the greatest refreshment to the spirits of man; without which, buildings and palaces are but gross handyworks. *For this month he recommended:* The double white violet; the wallflower; the stock gillyflower; the cowslip; flower de luces, and lilies of all natures; rosemary flowers; the tulip; the double peony; the pale daffodil; the French honeysuckle; the cherry tree in blossom; the damsin, and plum trees in blossom.

APRIL 2

APRIL 3   *Gerard Manley Hopkins was a Jesuit priest who wrote wonderful modern poetry. I don't fuss about his exact meaning: I just let the words roll into my mind and feel (rather than understand) their beauty.*

Nothing is so beautiful as spring –
When weeds, in wheels, shoot long and lovely and lush;
Thrush's eggs look little low heavens, and thrush
Through the echoing timber does so rinse and wring
The ear, it strikes like lightenings to hear him sing;
The glassy peartree leaves and blooms, they brush
The descending blue; that blue is all in a rush
With richness; the racing lambs too have fair their fling.

APRIL 4   Looking round on the noisy inanity of the world, words with little meaning, actions with little worth, one loves to reflect on the great empire of silence. The noble silent men, scattered here and there each in his department; silently thinking, silently working; whom no morning newspaper makes mention of! *A comforting thought from the Victorian writer, Thomas Carlyle, for days when the news seems depressing.*

APRIL

Of our voices we can frame
A ladder, if we will but tread
Beneath our feet each deed of shame.

All common things, each day's events,
That with the hour begin and end,
Our pleasures and our discontents,
Are rounds by which we may ascend.

The heights by great men reached and kept
Were not attained by sudden flight,
But they, while their companions slept,
Were toiling upward in the night.

HENRY WADSWORTH LONGFELLOW

My father used to recite this verse by Adam Lindsay Gordon, an Australian poet, to me when I was a child.

Life is mostly froth and bubble,
Only two things stand like stone
Kindness in another's trouble,
Courage in your own.

The bliss of the animals lies in this, that on their lower level, they shadow the bliss of those – few at any moment on the earth – who do not 'look before and after and pine for what is not' but live in the holy carelessness of the eternal now.

GEORGE MACDONALD

APRIL 8

Beauty still walketh on the earth and air . . .
The roses of the spring are ever fair;
'Mong branches green, still ring-doves coo and pair,
And the deep sea still foams its music old.
So, if we are at all divinely souled,
This beauty will unloose our bonds of care.

These lines by Robert Southey remind me to turn from my daily worries and refresh myself with beauty.

APRIL 9

As you love yourself, so shall you love others. Strange, but true, but with no exceptions. *This saying comes from Harry Stack Sullivan, an American psychiatrist who was wise in human relationships. It's food for thought.*

APRIL 10

I repeat the words of this hymn to myself when I am getting in too much of a rush and hurry. It is by John Greenleaf Whittier, the American Quaker poet.

Drop thy still dews of quietness
Till our all striving cease;
Take from our souls the strain and stress,
And let our ordered lives confess
The beauty of thy peace.

APRIL 11

If we turn our minds towards the good, it is impossible that little by little the whole soul will not be attracted thereto in spite of itself.

SIMONE WEIL

John Clare knew sorrow and despair first hand. Out of his unhappiness he wrote this poem about hope. APRIL 12

> Is there another world for this frail dust
> To warm with life and be itself again?
> Something about me daily speaks there must
> And why should instinct nourish hopes in vain?
> 'Tis nature's prophecy that such will be,
> And everything seems struggling to explain
> The closed sealed volume of its mystery.
> Time wandering onward keeps its usual pace,
> As seeming anxious of eternity,
> To meet that calm and find a resting place.
> E'en the small violet feels a future power
> And waits each year renewing blooms to bring;
> And surely man is no inferior flower
> To die unworthy of a second spring.

Somewhere in the Black Forest of Germany, there is a rough wooden cross with a seat below it. On the cross is written: Joy to him who comes. Peace to him who stays a while. Blessing on him who goes on his way. APRIL 13

APRIL 14   *Today is Cuckoo Day in Britain, the time when the cuckoo arrives promising summer is coming. Thomas Hardy's poem is full of optimism too.*

> This is the weather the cuckoo likes,
> And so do I;
> When showers betumble the chestnut spikes
> And nestlings fly:
> And the little brown nightingale bills his best,
> And they sit outside at 'The Traveller's Rest'
> And maids come forth spring-muslin drest,
> And citizens dream of the south and the west,
> And so do I.

APRIL 15   *On this day in 1802, Dorothy Wordsworth, the sister of the poet William Wordsworth, wrote this in her journal.*

We saw a few daffodils close to the water side . . . As we went along there were more and yet more . . . They grew among the mossy stones about and about them; some rested their heads upon these stones as on a pillow for weariness and the rest tossed and reeled and danced and seemed as if they verily laughed with the wind that blew upon them.

APRIL

APRIL 16

Her diary entry inspired her brother William Wordsworth to write a poem. Here are my two favourite verses.

> I wandered lonely as a cloud
> That floats on high o'er vales and hills,
> When all at once I saw a crowd,
> A host, of golden daffodils;
> Beside the lake, beneath the trees,
> Fluttering and dancing in the breeze.
>
> For oft, when on my couch I lie
> In vacant or in pensive mood,
> They flash upon that inward eye
> Which is the bliss of solitude;
> And then my heart with pleasure fills,
> And dances with the daffodils.

APRIL 17

What lies behind us and what lies before us are tiny matters compared to what lies within us.

RALPH WALDO EMERSON

APRIL 18

Courage is fear that has said its prayers.

PROVERB

APRIL 19

There is no duty we so much underrate as the duty of being happy. By being happy we sow anonymous benefits upon the world.

ROBERT LOUIS STEVENSON

APRIL 20   As the art of life is learned, it will be found at last that all lovely things are also necessary: the wild flower by the wayside, as well as the tended corn; and wild birds and creatures of the forest, as well as the tended cattle: because man doth not live by bread alone, but also by the desert manna; by every wondrous word and unknowable work of God. *Wrote John Ruskin, the Victorian critic.*

APRIL 21   Laughter is the nearest you can get to God.

SARAH MILES

APRIL 22   In judging others we can see too well
Their grievous fall, but not how grieved they fell;
Judging ourselves, we to our minds recall
Not how we fell, but how we grieved to fall.

GEORGE CRABBE

APRIL 23   *Today is the saint's day of St George, the dragon slayer, a day to recall the words of Reverend Sydney Smith.*

It is the greatest and the first use of history, to show us the sublime in morals, and to tell us what great men have done in perilous seasons. Such beings, and such actions, dignify our nature, and breathe into us a virtuous pride which is the parent of every good. Wherever you meet with them in the page of history, read them, mark them, and learn from them, how to live, and how to die!

APRIL

Of all the beasts, a dog is the only animal that, leaving his fellows, attempts to cultivate the friendship of man; to man he looks in all his necessities with a speaking eye for assistance; exerts for him all the little service in his power with cheerfulness and pleasure; for him bears famine and fatigue with patience and resignation; no injuries can abate his fidelity; no distress induce him to forsake his benefactor; studious to please, and fearing to offend, he is still an humble steadfast dependent, and in him alone fawning is not flattery. *Wrote the eighteenth-century man of letters, Oliver Goldsmith. We can learn from man's most loyal and cheerful friend.*

Laurens van der Post, the South African writer admired by the British *Prince of Wales, was being interviewed about his past life when he said:* An individual must not wait for governments and he must not wait for groups and powerful people to do something. He must take care of what is on his doorstep . . . You do what is necessary at a given moment with all your heart and all your soul.

APRIL 26   Contact with children teaches us sincerity, simplicity, the ability to live in the present hour, the present action. Children are, in a sense, reborn daily: hence their spontaneity, the lack of complexity in their souls, the simplicity of their judgements and actions. Moreover their intuitive distinctions between good and evil are direct and straightforward, their souls are free of the bonds of sin, they are not continually judging and analyzing.

FATHER ELCHANINOV

APRIL 27   This family affection, how good and beautiful it is! Men and maids love, and after many years they may rise to this. It is the grand proof of the goodness in human nature, for it means that the more we see of each other, the more we find that is lovable. If you would cease to dislike a man, try to get nearer his heart.

We often take family affection for granted, but the writer of these words, J. M. Barrie, creator of the boy who never grew up, Peter Pan, never had children of his own. Perhaps that is why he saw the value of family love so clearly.

There is a jewel which no Indian mines
Can buy, no chemic art can counterfeit;
It makes men rich in greatest poverty,
Makes water wine, turns wooden cups to gold,
The homely whistle to sweet music's strain;
Seldom it comes, to few from heaven sent,
That much in little, all in naught, Content.

ANONYMOUS

APRIL 28

My friend Danny Breslin from Florida tells the story of two men who were sitting on a bench in London's Hyde Park. They wanted to go shopping in Oxford St. One of them got up and started walking in the wrong direction, but he asked the way and a passerby put him right. He finally arrived at the shops but the other man just stayed on the bench. 'That guy who was walking in the wrong direction, was on his way. Even his mistake was part of getting there. The guy on the bench got nowhere. So if it feels right, give it a whirl,' *says Danny.*

APRIL 29

I am very fond of the poems of Robert Southwell, a martyred Catholic priest in Elizabethan England.

APRIL 30

Shun delays, they breed remorse,
Take thy time, while time is lent thee;
Creeping snails have weakest force,
Fly their fault, lest thou repent thee:
Good is best when soonest wrought,
Lingering labour comes to nought.

MAY

MAY 1

For May Morning the poet John Milton wrote this song three centuries ago, marking the start of summer.

Now the bright morning star, day's harbinger,
Comes dancing from the East, and leads with her
The flowery May, who from her green lap throws
The yellow cowslip and the pale primrose.
Hail bounteous May! that dost inspire
Mirth and youth and warm desire;
Woods and groves are of thy dressing
Hill and dale doth boast thy blessing.
Thus we salute thee with our early song,
And welcome thee, and wish thee long.

MAY 2

Sometimes at breakfast, sometimes in a train or empty bus, or on the moving stairs at Charing Cross, I am happy; the earth turns to gold, and life becomes a magical adventure. Only yesterday, travelling alone to Sussex, I became light-headed with this sudden joy. The train seemed to rush to its adorable destination through a world new-born in splendour, bathed in a beautiful element, fresh and clear as on the morning of Creation. *These moments of intense joy, described by the American essayist Logan Pearsall Smith, do not depend on the beauty of the countryside; they can happen to us anywhere, if we are open to them.*

MAY 3

It is not growing like a tree
In bulk, doth make man better be;
Or standing long an oak, three hundred year,
To fall a log at last, dry, bald and sere:
A lily of a day
Is fairer far in May,
Although it fall and die that night –
It was the plant and flower of light.
In small proportions we just beauty see;
And in short measures life may perfect be.

BEN JONSON

MAY 4

Be kind and merciful. Let no one ever come to you without leaving better and happier. Be the living expression of God's kindness: kindness in your face, kindness in your smile, kindness in your warm greeting. In the slums we are the light of God's kindness to the poor. To children, to the poor, to all who suffer and are lonely, give always a happy smile. Give them not only your care, but also your heart.

MOTHER TERESA OF CALCUTTA

MAY

MAY 5

One of my favourite passages in the Bible comes from Paul's Epistle to the Romans, in which he promises:

Neither death, nor life, nor principalities, nor powers, nor things present, nor things to come, nor height, nor depth, nor any other creature, shall be able to separate us from the love of God.

MAY 6

A little child He took for sign
To them that sought the way divine.
And once a flower sufficed to show
The whole of that we need to know.
Now here we lie, the child and I,
And watch the clouds go floating by,
Just telling stories turn by turn . . .
Lord, which is teacher, which doth learn.

H. D. Lowry

MAY 7

The only real failure in life is giving up. On looking back let it stand to our credit in life's balance sheet that at least we tried, and tried hard.

An inspiring thought from the countryman A. G. Street.

MAY 8

He prayeth best who loveth best
All things both great and small,
For the dear God who loveth us,
He made and loveth all.

Samuel Coleridge

MAY 9   *Rudyard Kipling is such a wise poet. He writes about things which concern us all, like this poem about letting others go their own way in life.*

> In faiths and food and books and friends
> Give every soul her choice.
> For such as follow divers ends
> In diverse lights rejoice.
>
> There is a glory in all things;
> But each must find his own,
> Sufficient for his reckonings,
> Which is to him alone.

MAY 10   Sow and act, and you reap a habit. Sow a habit, and you reap a character. Sow a character, and you reap a destiny.

CHARLES READE

MAY 11   There is so much good in the worst of us,
> And so much bad in the best of us,
> That it hardly becomes any of us
> To talk about the rest of us.

This is a wise little verse from an unknown author. But what is said is painfully true.

MAY 12   A candle lights others and consumes itself.

JEWISH SAYING

MAY

MAY 13

There is a motto, Let Go and Let God. Someone gave me this prose poem by an unknown author. It suggests how we can use the motto to live happier lives. We should try to accept life and leave the outcome to God.

To let go is not to adjust everything to my own desires –
But to take each day as it comes and cherish myself in it.

To let go is not to regret the past –
But to grow and live for the future.

To let go is to fear less – and to love more.

MAY 14

There is, perhaps, a special pleasure in re-learning the names of many of the flowers every spring. It is like re-reading a book that one has almost forgotten ... Once more I shall see the world as a garden through the eyes of a stranger, my breath taken away with surprise by the painted fields.

ROBERT LYND

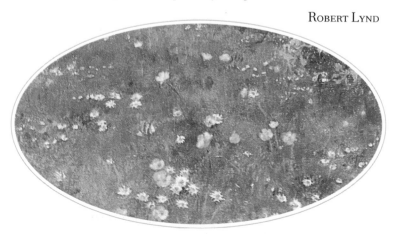

MAY 15

Spring goeth all in white,
Crowned with milk-white may;
In fleecy flocks of light
O'er heaven the white clouds stray.

White butterflies in the air;
White daisies prank the ground;
The cherry and the hoary pear
Scatter their snow around.

ROBERT BRIDGES

MAY 16 We dull our understandings with trifles, waste the heavenly time with hurry. When I trouble myself over a trifle, – the loss of some little article, say – spurring my memory, and hunting the house, not from immediate need, but from dislike of loss: when a book has been borrowed of me and not returned, and I have forgotten the borrower, and fret over the missing volume . . . is it not time I lost a few things when I care for them so unreasonably?

GEORGE MACDONALD

He who wants to keep his garden tidy, doesn't reserve a plot for weeds.

MAY 17

DAG HAMMARSKJOLD

If I have faltered more or less
In my great task of happiness;
If I have moved among my race
And shown no glorious morning face;
If beams from happy human eyes
Have moved me not; if morning skies,
Books, and my food, and summer rain
Knocked on my sullen heart in vain; –
Lord, Thy most pointed pleasure take
And stab my spirit broad awake.

MAY 18

ROBERT LOUIS STEVENSON

Always you have been told that work is a curse and labour a misfortune.
But I say to you that when you work you fulfil a part of earth's furthest dream, assigned to you when that dream was born.

MAY 19

Kahlil Gibran was a Lebanese poet from whose poem The Prophet these inspiring lines are taken.

The more we love, the better we are, and the greater our friendships are, the dearer we are to God.

MAY 20

JEREMY TAYLOR

MAY

MAY 21   Look to this day ... In it lies all the realities and verities of existence, the bliss of growth, the splendour of action, the glory of power. For yesterday is but a dream and tomorrow is only a vision. But today, well lived, makes every yesterday a dream of happiness and every tomorrow a vision of hope.

A SANSKRIT PROVERB

MAY 22   Keep the faculty of effort alive in you by a little gratuitous exercise every day. That is, be systematically heroic in little unnecessary points, do every day or two something for no other reason than its difficulty.

WILLIAM JAMES

MAY 23

Then gently scan your brother man,
Still gentler sister woman;
Tho' they may gang a kennin wrang
To step aside is human;
One point must still be greatly dark –
The moving *why* they do it;
And just as lamely can ye mark
How far perhaps they rue it.

This plea for forgiveness is by Robert Burns

MAY 24   It were not best that we should all think alike.

MARK TWAIN

MAY

MAY 25

These lovely lines by William Blake were written 200 years ago and yet are as true today as then.

> A robin redbreast in a cage
> Puts all heaven in a rage.
> A dovehouse filled with doves and pigeons
> Shudders hell through all its regions.
> A dog starved at his master's gate
> Predicts the ruin of the state.

MAY 26

Walk in the fields in one of the mornings of May, and if you carry with you a mind unpolluted with harm, watch how it is impressed. You are delighted with the beauty of colours; are not those colours beautiful? You see the sun rising from behind a mountain and the heavens painted with light; is not that renewal of the light of the morning sublime? You reject all obvious reasons, and say that these things are beautiful and sublime, because the accidents of life have made them so; I say they are beautiful and sublime because God has made them so!

SYDNEY SMITH

<u>MAY 27</u>

Love lives beyond
The tomb, the earth, which fades like dew!
I love the fond,
The faithful and the true.

Love lives in sleep,
The happiness of healthy dreams:
Eve's dews may weep
But love delightful seems.

'Tis seen in flowers
And in the morning's pearly dew;
In earth's green hours
And in the heaven's eternal blue.

JOHN CLARE

<u>MAY 28</u> Your enjoyment of the world is never right till every morning
you awake in heaven, see yourself in your Father's palace, and
look upon the skies and the earth and the air as celestial joys.

THOMAS TRAHERNE

MAY

MAY 29

Today is oak leaf day, a good time for a passage by Richard Jefferies, one of the greatest nature writers.

I must stay under the old tree in the midst of the long grass. I seem as if I could feel all the glowing life the sunshine gives and the south wind calls to being. The endless grass, the endless leaves, the immense strength of the oak expanding, the unalloyed joy of finch and blackbird; from all of them I receive a little. Each gives me something of the pure joy they gather for themselves. To be beautiful and to be calm, without mental fear, is the ideal of nature. If I cannot achieve it, at least I can think it.

MAY 30

A blessing on the flowers
That God has made so good,
From crops of jealous gardens
To wildlings of a wood.

CHRISTINA ROSSETTI

MAY 31

Where do you get the strength to go on, when you have used up all of your own strength? Where do you turn for patience when you have run out of patience, when you have been more patient for more years than anyone should be asked to be, and the end is nowhere in sight? I believe that God gives us strength and patience and hope, renewing our spiritual resources when they run dry.

HAROLD S. KUSHNER

JUNE

O June, O June, that we desired so,
Wilt though not make us happy on this day?
Across the river thy soft breezes blow
Sweet with the scent of beanfields far away,
Above our heads rustle the aspens grey,
Calm is the sky with harmless clouds beset,
No thought of storm the morning vexes yet.

WILLIAM MORRIS

JUNE 1

One of the great principles of life is the 'As if' principle also known as the 'Fake it to make it' idea. We come across this in the writings of the American psychologist and philosopher William James.

JUNE 2

The sovereign voluntary path to cheerfulness, if our spontaneous cheerfulness be lost, is to sit up cheerfully, and to act and speak as if cheerfulness were already there. If such conduct does not make you soon feel cheerful, nothing else on that occasion can. So to feel brave, act as if we *were* brave, use all our will to that end, and a courage-fit will very likely replace the fit of fear. Again, in order to feel kindly toward a person to whom we have been inimical, the only way is more or less deliberately to smile, to make sympathetic inquiries, and to force ourselves to say genial things.

JUNE 3

My favourite poem about home is by John Clare.
Like a thing of the desert alone it its glee
I make a small home seem an empire to me.
Like a bird in the forest whose home is its nest,
My home is my all and the centre of rest.
Let ambition stride over the world at a stride,
Let the restless go rolling away with the tide,
I look on Life's pleasures as follies at best,
And like sunset, feel calm when I'm going to rest.

I walk round the orchard on sweet summer eves
And rub the perfume from the blackcurrant leaves
Which like the geranium when touched leaves a smell
That lad's love and sweet briar can hardly excel;
And watch the things grow all begemed with the shower
That glitter like pearls in a sunshiny hour,
And hear the pert robin just startle a tune
To cheer the lone hedger when labour is done.

JUNE 4

Humour is mankind's greatest blessing.

MARK TWAIN

JUNE

Whenever I have found that I have blundered or that my work has been imperfect, and when I have been contemptuously criticised and even when I have been overpraised, so that I have felt mortified, it has been my greatest comfort to say hundreds of times to myself that 'I have worked as hard and as well as I could, and no man can do more than this.'

CHARLES DARWIN

> Happy the man, whose wish and care
> A few paternal acres bound,
> Content to breathe his native air,
>   In his own ground.
>
> Blest, who can unconcern'dly find
> Hours, days and years slide soft away,
> In health of body, peace of mind,
>   Quiet by day.
>
> Sound sleep by night; study and ease,
> Together mixt; sweet recreation:
> And innocence, which most does please
>   With meditation

ALEXANDER POPE

Do not believe that all greatness and heroism are in the past. Learn to discover princes, prophets, heroes and saints among the people about you. Be assured they are there. *This rule for life comes from the American scholar and philosopher Thomas Davidson.*

JUNE 8

Be strong to hope, O heart.
Though day is bright,
The stars can only shine
In the dark night.
Be strong, O heart of mine,
Look towards the light!

ADELAIDE PROCTOR

JUNE 9 The exceeding beauty of the earth yields a new thought with every petal. The hours when the mind is absorbed by beauty are the only hours when we really live. *The writer Richard Jefferies clung to this belief.*

JUNE 10 *An old French verse translated here is so true!*

Some of your griefs you have cured,
And the sharpest you will have survived;
But what torments of pain you endured
From the evils that never arrived!

JUNE 11 Once in an age, God sends to some of us a friend who loves in us, not a false imagining, an unreal character – but, looking through all the rubbish of our imperfections, loves in us the divine ideal of our nature – loves not the man that we are, but the angel that we may be. Such friends seem inspired by a divine gift of prophecy.

HARRIET BEECHER STOWE

JUNE

JUNE 12

Imperfection is in some sort essential to all that we know of life. It is the sign of life in a mortal body. Nothing that lives is, or can be, rigidly perfect. The foxglove blossom – a third part bud, a third part past, a third part in full bloom – is a type of the life of this world. And in all things that live there are certain irregularities and deficiencies which are not only signs of life but sources of beauty. No human face is exactly the same in its lines on each side, no leaf perfect in its lobes, no branch in its symmetry. All admit irregularity as they imply change; and to banish imperfection is to destroy expression. All things are literally better, lovelier, and more beloved for the imperfections which have been divinely appointed.

JOHN RUSKIN

JUNE 13

Small service is true service while it lasts:
Of humblest friends, bright creature, scorn not one:
The daisy, by the shadow that it casts,
Protects the lingering dew-drop from the sun.

William Wordsworth wrote out this little verse in the album of a small child in 1834.

JUNE

JUNE 14   *Bishop George Appleton wrote this prayer for animals.*
O God, I thank thee
for all the creatures thou hast made, so perfect in
     their kind –
great animals like the elephant and rhinoceros,
humorous animals like the camel and the monkey,
friendly ones like the dog and the cat,
working ones like the horse and the ox,
timid ones like the squirrel and the rabbit,
majestic ones like the lion and tiger,
for birds with their songs.
O Lord give us such love for thy creation
that love may cast out fear,
and all thy creatures see in man
their priest and friend,
through Jesus Christ our Lord.

JUNE 15   Deeds of kindness weigh as much as all the commandments.

THE TALMUD

JUNE

JUNE 16

When I am downcast, when I am unhappy with myself, I recall this wise Jewish saying, which cheers me up.

If a man is cruel to himself, how can we expect him to be compassionate to others?

JUNE 17

O gift of God! O perfect day:
Whereon shall no man work, but play;
Whereon it is enough for me,
Not to be doing, but to be.

HENRY WADSWORTH LONGFELLOW

JUNE 18

What sensation is so delightful as Hope? and if it were not for Hope, where would the future be? – in hell. It is useless to say where the present is, for most of us know: and as for the past, what predominates in memory? – Hope baffled. Ergo, in all human affairs, it is Hope – Hope – Hope.
Lord Byron wrote this in 1821 in his journal.

JUNE 19

The rose is fairest when 'tis budding new,
And hope is brightest when it dawns from fears,
The rose is sweetest washed in morning dew,
And love is loveliest when embalmed in tears.
O, wilding rose, whom fancy thus endears,
I bid your blossoms in my bonnet wave,
Emblem of hope and love through future years.

SIR WALTER SCOTT

JUNE 20   If we except those miraculous and isolated moments fate can bestow on a man, loving your work (unfortunately, the privilege of a few) represents the best, most concrete approximation of happiness on earth. But this is a truth not many know.

PRIMO LEVI

JUNE 21

Hope is the thing with feathers
That perches in the soul,
And sings the tune without the words,
And never stops at all.

And sweetest in the gale is heard,
And sore must be the storm
That could abash the little bird
That kept so many warm.

I like the way the American poet Emily Dickinson compares hope to a bird, comforting us in bad times.

JUNE 22   To say there is no path, because we have often got into the wrong path, puts an end to all other knowledge as well as to this.

SYDNEY SMITH

JUNE 23

Ah, but a man's reach should exceed his grasp,
Or what's a heaven for?

ROBERT BROWNING

When all's done, all tried, all counted here,
All great arts, and all good philosophies,
This love puts its hand out in a dream
And straight outstretches all things.

JUNE 24

ELIZABETH BARRETT BROWNING

These roses under my window make no reference to former roses or to better ones; they are for what they are; they exist with God today. There is no time to them. There is simply the rose; it is perfect in every moment of its existence. Before a leaf-bud has burst, its whole life acts; in the full-blown flower there is no more; in the leafless root there is no less. Its nature is satisfied, and it satisfies nature, in all moments alike. But man postpones or remembers; he does not live in the present, but with reverted eye laments the past, or, heedless of the riches that surround him, stands on tiptoe to foresee the future. He cannot be happy and strong until he too lives with nature in the present, above time.

JUNE 25

RALPH WALDO EMERSON

JUNE 26 *The French pilot and novelist Antoine de Saint-Exupery wrote the parable of The Little Prince the year before his death in 1944. It tells the tale of a pilot who crashes his plane in the desert where he meets a little prince from another world.*

'The men where you live,' said the little prince, 'raise five thousand roses in the same garden – and they do not find in it what they are looking for.'

'They do not find it,' I replied.

'And yet what they are looking for could be found in a single rose or in a little water.'

'Yes, that is true,' I said.

And the little prince added:

'But the eyes are blind. One must look with the heart ...'

JUNE 27 *The great protestant reformer Martin Luther also marvelled at the beauty of a rose which we take for granted. He said:* 'Tis a magnificent work of God: could a man make but one such rose as this, he would be thought worthy of all honour, but the gifts of God lose their value in our eyes from their very infinity.

JUNE

Precious pearls and jewels, and far more precious truth are found in muddy shells and places. The rich mines of golden truth lie hid under barren hills and in obscure holes and corners.

Roger Williams, a minister in New England, was in favour of religious toleration partly for this reason – that we may learn something from unexpected people.

Oh yet we trust that somehow good
Will be the final goal of ill,
To pangs of nature, sins of will,
Defects of doubt, and taints of blood.

That nothing walks with aimless feet;
That not one life shall be destroyed,
Or cast as rubbish to the void,
When God hath made the pile complete;

That not a worm is cloven in vain;
That not a moth with vain desire
Is shrivelled in a fruitless fire,
Or but subserves another's gain.

ALFRED LORD TENNYSON

Knowledge which helps reform the heart, is of much more use to us than that which only enlightens the understanding.

BISHOP THOMAS WILSON

JULY

All things that love the sun are out of doors;
The sky rejoices in the morning's birth;
The grass is bright with rain-drops; – on the moors
The hare is running races in her mirth;
And with her feet she from the plashy earth
Raises a mist; that, glittering in the sun,
Runs with her all the way, wherever she doth run.

WILLIAM WORDSWORTH

Love is a great thing and a good, and alone maketh heavy burdens light, and beareth in like balance things pleasant and unpleasant; it beareth a heavy burden and feeleth it not, and maketh bitter things to be savoury and sweet. Love will always have his mind upward to God and will not be occupied with love of the world. Nothing, therefore, is more sweet than love, nothing higher, nothing stronger, nothing larger, nothing more joyful, nothing fuller, nor anything better in heaven or earth; for love descendeth from God, and may not rest finally in anything lower than God. *This lovely passage about the powers of love was written by St Thomas à Kempis, a medieval monk who wrote the Imitation of Christ, a well-known book of Christian devotion.*

<u>JULY 3</u> *Today is the first of the 'dog days' so called because the dog star rises and sets with the sun during this time. The novelist John Galsworthy wrote:* There are innumerable people in all ranks of the civilised world who would echo the words I heard last night: 'If I were condemned to spend twenty-four hours alone with a single creature, I would choose to spend them with my dog.' There is a quiet comfort in the companionship of a dog with its ever-ready touching humility, which human companionship, save of the nearest, does not bring.

<u>JULY 4</u>   Hope, whose eyes
Can sound the seas unsoundable, the skies
Inaccessible of eyesight; that can see
What earth beholds not, hear what wind and sea
Hear not, and speak what all these crying in one
Can speak not to the sun.

These lines on the powers of hope come from the Victorian poet, Algernon Swinburne. Hope, like faith and love, brings miracles in ordinary lives.

JULY

I am certain of nothing but the holiness of the heart's affections and the truth of imagination – what imagination seizes as beauty must be truth, *wrote the poet John Keats to one of his friends.*

. . . Let us be content, in work,
To do the thing we can, and not presume
To fret because it's little.

ELIZABETH BARRETT BROWNING

True contentment is a thing as active as agriculture. It is the power of getting out of any situation all that there is in it. It is arduous and it is rare. The absence of this digestive talent is what makes so cold and incredible the tales of so many people, who say they have been 'through' things; when it is evident that they have come out on the other side quite unchanged.

I like G. K. Chesterton's idea of contentment as an active virtue and I try hard to put it into practice.

From that wise mystic poet William Blake comes this verse that looks right into the human heart.

I was angry with my friend:
I told my wrath, my wrath did end.
I was angry with my foe:
I told it not, my wrath did grow.

JULY 9   Just as your hand, held before the eye, can hide the tallest mountain, so this small earthly life keeps us from seeing the vast radiance that fills the core of the Universe.

This thought comes from an eighteenth-century Jewish teacher, Rabbi Nachman of Bratslaw.

JULY 10   The most complete and healthy sleep that can be taken in the day is in summer time, out on a field. There is, perhaps, no solitary sensation so exquisite as that of slumbering on the grass or hay, shaded from the hot sun by a tree, with the consciousness of a fresh but light air running through the wide atmosphere, and the sky stretching far overhead upon all sides. Earth, and heaven, and a placid humanity seem to have the creation to themselves.

LEIGH HUNT

JULY 11

In this short life
That only lasts an hour,
How much – how little – is
Within our power.

EMILY DICKINSON

JULY 12   *A friend gave me a card with this modern version of the familiar words of St Matthew's Gospel. I read them and realised how comforting they were.*

Are not two sparrows sold for a penny? Yet not one of them will fall to the ground apart from the will of your Father. And even the very hairs of your head are numbered. So don't be afraid; you are worth more than many sparrows.

JULY

How many things might be tolerated in peace and left to conscience, had we but charity, and were it not the chief stronghold of our hypocrisy to be ever judging one another.

JOHN MILTON

This little Victorian verse about flowers is framed and hangs in the house of a keen gardener.

Our outward life requires them not,
Then wherefore had they birth?
To minister delight to men,
To beautify the earth:
To comfort man, to whisper hope,
Whene'er his faith is dim:
For who so careth for the flowers
Will much more care for him.

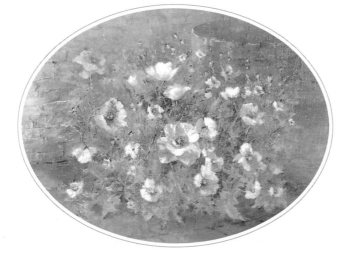

JULY 15

Trees grow, not alike,
    by the mound and the moat;
Birds sing in the forest
    with varying note;
Of the fish in the river
    some dive and some float.
The mountains rise high
    and the waters sink low,
But the why and the wherefore
    we never can know.

This is a translation of a Chinese poem written more than 1,500 years ago by Hsiao Yen. It reminds me to accept the differences in other people with joy.

JULY 16   The next hour, the next moment, is as much beyond our grasp and as much in God's care, as that a hundred years away. Care for the next minute is just as foolish as care for the morrow, or for a day in the next thousand years – in neither can we do anything, in both God is doing everything.

GEORGE MACDONALD

JULY

Life has no pleasure higher or nobler than that of friendship.   JULY 17

Little drops of water,   JULY 18
Little grains of sand,
Make the mighty ocean
And the beauteous land.

Little deeds of kindness,
Little words of love,
Make our earth an Eden
Like the heaven above.

Many children were taught this poem by Mrs J. A. Carney: it isn't great verse but it is great truth.

Die when I may, I want it said of me by those who knew me   JULY 19
best, that I always plucked a thistle and planted a flower,
where I thought a flower would grow.

ABRAHAM LINCOLN

Let us then be up and doing,   JULY 20
With a heart for any fate;
Still achieving, still pursuing,
Learn to labour and to wait.

HENRY WADSWORTH LONGFELLOW

JULY 21   *Today is the date of the death of Robert Burns, Scotland's great poet who spoke for all men.*

> What though on hamely fare we dine,
> Wear hoddin grey, an' a' that?
> Gie fools their silks, and knaves their wine,
> A man's a man for a' that
> For a' that, an' a' that,
> Their tinsel show an' a' that,
> The honest man, tho' e'er sae poor,
> Is king o' men for a' that.

JULY 22   We are too ready to retaliate rather than to forgive or to gain by love and information. Let us, then, try what love will do: for if men do once see we love them, we should soon find they would not harm us.

WILLIAM PENN

JULY 23   Great God, I ask thee for no meaner pelf,
> Than that I may not disappoint myself,
> That in my action I may soar as high,
> As I can now discern with this clear eye . . .
> That my weak hand may equal my firm faith,
> And my life practise more than my tongue saith.

HENRY DAVID THOREAU

JULY 24   God is a busy worker but he loves help.

BASQUE PROVERB

JULY

A good and wholesome thing is a little harmless fun in this world; it tones a body up and keeps him human and prevents him from souring.

It's the sharp common sense of Mark Twain that I enjoy – yes, all work and no play can sour people.

Brown butterflies in happy quiet rest
Upon the blooming ragwort's golden breast,
Giving unto the mind a sweet employ
That everything in nature meets with joy.
Ah sweet indeed! For trifles such as these
Full often give my aching bosom ease,
When I am in little walks my mind employ
Aright – and feel those happy reveries
That nature in her varied lessons tend
To bring our thinkings to a happy end,
And in her varied moods for ever tries
To make us that great blessing comprehend,
That spreads around us in a fond caress
Emblems and moods of future happiness.

JOHN CLARE

JULY 27   The Lord is my shepherd; I shall not want.
He maketh me to lie down in green pastures: He
leadeth me beside the still waters.
He restoreth my soul; He leadeth me in the paths of
righteousness for His name's sake.
Yea, though I walk through the valley of the shadow
of death, I will fear no evil: for Thou art with me:
Thy rod and Thy staff they comfort me.
Thou preparest a table before me in the presence of
mine enemies: Thou anointest my head with oil: my
cup runneth over.
Surely goodness and mercy shall follow me all the
days of my life: and I will dwell in the house of the
Lord for ever.

PSALM 23

JULY 28   Who is there that can make muddy water clear? But if allowed
to remain still, it will gradually become clear of itself... Be
sparing of speech, and things will come right of themselves.

LAO-TZU

All beauty warms the heart, is a sign of health, prosperity and the favour of God. What delights, what emancipates, not what scares and pains us, is wise and good in speech and in the arts. For, truly, the heart at the centre of the universe with every throb hurls the flood of happiness into every artery, vein, and veinlet, so that the whole system is inundated with the tides of joy.

RALPH WALDO EMERSON

JULY 29

These are things, that being possessed
Will make a life that's truly blessed:
No strife, warm clothes, a quiet soul,
A strength entire, a body whole,
Prudent simplicity, equal friends,
A diet that no art commends.
A night not drunk and yet secure;
A bed not sad, yet chaste and pure.
Long sleeps to make the nights but short,
A will to be but what thou art.

THOMAS RANDOLPH

JULY 30

The writer Katherine Mansfield had this to say about the fear that holds us back from trying. Fear of failure is worse than failure itself.

When we begin to take our failures non-seriously, it means we are ceasing to be afraid of them. It is of immense importance to learn to laugh at ourselves.

JULY 31

AUGUST

Today is Lammas Day (the word is from Loafmass), the day for *celebrating the gift of corn. John Donne, both poet and Dean of St Paul's in the seventeenth century wrote in one of his sermons:*

God made sun and moon to distinguish seasons, and day, and night, and we cannot have the fruits of the earth but in their seasons. But God hath made no decree to distinguish the seasons of his mercies. In paradise the fruits were ripe the first minute, and in heaven it is always autumn, his mercies are ever in their maturity. We ask our daily bread, and God never says you should have come yesterday, He never says you must again tomorrow, but today if you will hear His voice, today He will hear you.

Though hope is one of the three great virtues, poets often ignore it in *favour of love! One exception is Thomas Campbell who wrote a long poem about hope from which come these charming lines.*

> Auspicious Hope! in thy sweet garden grow
> Wreaths for each toil, a charm for every woe.
> Won by their sweets, in Nature's languid hour
> The way-worn pilgrim seeks thy summer bower.
> There, as the wild bee murmurs on the wind,
> What peaceful dreams thy handmaid-spirits bring!

AUGUST 3

There is a pleasure in the pathless woods,
There is a rapture on the lonely shore,
There is society where none intrudes,
By the deep Sea, and music in its roar;
I love not Man the less, but Nature more,
From these our interviews, in which I steal,
From all I may be or have been before,
To mingle with the universe, and feel
What I can ne'er express, yet cannot all conceal.

LORD BYRON

AUGUST 4

The value of friends is often forgotten in today's busy world. Ralph Waldo Emerson knew better.

Life goes headlong. We chase some flying scheme, or we are hunted by some fear or command behind us. But if suddenly we encounter a friend, we pause; our heat and hurry look foolish enough; now pause, now possession, is required, and the power to swell the moment from the resources of the heart. The moment is all, in all noble relations . . . A friend is the hope of the heart.

AUGUST

Surely there are in every man's life certain rubs, doublings and
wrenches, which pass awhile under the effects of chance, but
at the last, well examined, prove the mere hand of God.

Sir Thomas Browne

To see a world in a grain of sand
And heaven in a wild flower,
Hold infinity in the palm of your hand
And eternity in an hour.

William Blake

To accomplish great things we must not only act, but also
dream, not only plan, but also believe.

Anatole France

To suffer wrongs which hope thinks infinite;
To forgive wrongs darker than death or night;
To defy power, which seems omnipotent;
To love and bear; to hope till hope creates
From its own wreck the thing it contemplates;
Neither to change, nor falter, nor repent;
This, like thy glory, Titan, is to be
Good, great and joyous, beautiful and free.

*These lines come from a long poem, Prometheus Unbound, by Percy
Bysshe Shelley. It is the great soul that keeps on hoping when hope
seems dead.*

AUGUST 9   A parent must respect the spiritual person of his child and approach it with reverence, for that too looks the Father in the face and has an audience with Him into which no earthly parent can enter even if he dared desire it.

GEORGE MACDONALD

AUGUST 10   Mid pleasures and palaces though we may roam,
Be it ever so humble there's no place like home!
The charm from the skies seems to hallow us there,
Which seek through the world, is ne'er met with elsewhere.

J. HOWARD PAYNE

AUGUST 11   Great Spirit, grant that I may not criticize my neighbour until I have walked a mile in his moccasins.

I found this American Indian prayer on a postcard.

AUGUST 12   Here, in this little bay,
Full of tumultuous life and great repose,
Where, twice a day,
The purposeless, glad ocean comes and goes,
Under high cliffs, and far from the huge town,
I sit me down.
For want of me the world's course will not fail;
When all its work is done, the lie shall rot;
The truth is great, and shall prevail,
When none cares whether it prevail or not.

COVENTRY PATMORE

AUGUST

Joys come like the grass in the field springing there
Without the mere toil of attention and care.
They come of themselves like a star in the sky
And the brighter they shine when the cloud passes by.

JOHN CLARE

The great psychologist William James talked to people about their spiritual experiences. This is one anonymous farm worker's story.

When I went in the morning into the fields to work, the glory of God appeared in all His visible creation. I well remember we reaped oats, and how every straw and head of the oats seemed arrayed in a kind of rainbow glory, or to glow in the glory of God.

AUGUST 15   *This is my mother's favourite poem – a version of the 23rd psalm written by Joseph Addison.*

> The Lord my pasture shall prepare,
> And feed me with a shepherd's care;
> His presence shall my wants supply,
> And guard me with a watchful eye;
> My noonday walks he shall attend,
> And all my midnight hours defend.
>
> When in the sultry glebe I faint,
> Or on the thirsty mountain pant,
> To fertile walks and dewy meads
> My weary wandering steps he leads,
> Where peaceful rivers, soft and slow,
> Amid the verdant landscape flow.

AUGUST 16   The truth hurts like a thorn at first; but in the end it blossoms like a rose.

This is a wise saying of Samuel Ha-Nagid, a Jewish scholar who lived at the Arabic court of Granada a thousand years ago.

The rule for us all is perfectly simple. Do not waste time bothering whether you 'love' your neighbour; act as if you did. As soon as we do this we find one of the great secrets. When you are behaving as if you loved someone, you will presently come to love him.

C. S. LEWIS

Nature never did betray
The heart that loved her; 'tis her privilege,
Through all the years of this our life, to lead
From joy to joy.

WILLIAM WORDSWORTH

Socrates, the philosopher of ancient Greece, used to tell his followers to be what they would like to seem to be. The shortest, and safest, and best way is to strive to be really good, in that in which you wish to be thought good. Whatever are called virtues among mankind, you will find capable of being increased by study and exercise.

It isn't the thing you do, dear,
It's the thing you leave undone
Which gives you a bit of a heartache
At the setting of the sun.

MARGARET SANGSTER

AUGUST 21

Oh! when shall I 'scape to be truly my own,
From the noise and the smoke and the bustle of town.
Hail ye woods and ye lawns, shady vales, sunny hills,
And the warble of birds, and the murmur of rills.
I have said it at home, I have said it abroad,
That the town is man's world, but that this is of God.

ISAAC HAWKINS BROWNE

AUGUST 22

I have a simple philosophy. Fill what's empty.
Empty what's full. And scratch where it itches.

ALICE ROOSEVELT LONGWORTH

AUGUST 23

We that acquaint ourselves with every zone,
And pass the tropics and behold each pole,
When we come home are to ourselves unknown,
And unacquainted still with our own soul.

A thoughtful verse by Sir John Davies about the way we travel abroad or explore new places, only to forget that we hardly know our own selves.

AUGUST 24

I would rather make mistakes in kindness and compassion than work miracles in unkindness and hardness.

MOTHER TERESA OF CALCUTTA

AUGUST

Henry of Navarre, one of the greatest French kings, was about to go into his first battle at the age of 14. He was upset by the way his knees were trembling so he looked at them fiercely and said:

AUGUST 25

That's right, tremble, tremble! You would tremble a good deal more if you knew where I was taking you!

He is very imprudent, a dog is. He never makes it his business to inquire whether you are in the right or in the wrong, never bothers as to whether you are going up or down upon life's ladder, never asks whether you are rich or poor, silly or wise, sinner or saint. You are his pal. That is enough for him, and come luck or misfortune, good repute or bad, honour or shame, he is going to stick to you, to comfort you, guard you, give his life for you if need be. *These lovely words come from Jerome K. Jerome, author of Three Men in a Boat, and a man who was far-sighted enough to value the unconditional love and loyalty of an animal.*

AUGUST 26

AUGUST

AUGUST 27 The first time I read an excellent book, it is to me just as if I had gained a new friend. When I read over a book I have perused before, it resembles the meeting with an old one. A man never opens a book without reaping some advantage by it.

OLIVER GOLDSMITH

AUGUST 28

When by my solitary hearth I sit,
And hateful thoughts enwrap my soul in gloom;
When no fair dreams before my mind's eye flit,
And the bare heath of life presents no bloom;
Sweet Hope, ethereal balm upon me shed,
And wave thy silver pinions o'er my head.

Should Disappointment, parent of Despair,
Strive for her son to seize my careless heart;
When, like a cloud, he sits upon the air,
Preparing on his spellbound prey to dart:
Chase him away, sweet Hope, with visage bright
And fright him as the morning frightens night!

JOHN KEATS

AUGUST

AUGUST 29

Here is what Lao-Tʒu, a Chinese philosopher who lived six centuries before Christ, said about being humble. It is familar.

Follow diligently the Way in your own heart, but make no display of it to the world. Keep behind, and you shall be put in front; keep out, and you shall be kept in. He that humbles himself shall be preserved entire. He that bends shall be made straight. He that is empty shall be filled. He that is worn out shall be renewed.

AUGUST 30

Pluck not the wayside flower,
It is the traveller's dower;
A thousand passersby
Its beauties may espy,
May win a touch of blessing
From nature's mild caressing.

WILLIAM ALLINGHAM

AUGUST 31

Work is of a religious nature: – work is of a *brave* nature; which is the aim of all religion to be. All work of man is as the swimmer's; a waste ocean threatens to devour him; if he front it not bravely it will keep its word. By incessant wise defiance of it, lusty rebuke and buffet of it, behold how it loyally supports him, bears him as its conquerer along. It is so with all things that man undertakes in this world. *These words of good cheer at the end of the holiday time came from Thomas Carlyle.*

SEPTEMBER

Season of mist and mellow fruitfulness,
Close bosom-friend of the maturing sun;
Conspiring with him how to load and bless
With fruit the vines that round the thatch-eves run;
To bend with apples the moss'd cottage trees,
And fill all fruit with ripeness to the core;
To swell the gourd, and plump the hazel shells
With a sweet kernel; to set budding more,
And still more, later flowers for the bees,
Until they think warm days will never cease,
For summer has o'er-brimmed their clammy cells.

JOHN KEATS

SEPTEMBER 1

No outward changes of condition in life can keep the nightingale of its eternal meaning from singing in all sorts of different men's hearts. That is the main fact to remember. If we could not only admit it with our lips, but really and truly believe it, how our convulsive insistencies, how our antipathies and dreads of each other, would soften down! If the poor and the rich could look at each other in this way, how gentle would grow their disputes! what tolerance and good humour, what willingness to live and let live, would come into the world!

WILLIAM JAMES

SEPTEMBER 2

<u>SEPTEMBER 3</u> We talk of creation as a past thing. But the truth is, creation is eternal. Creation never ceases. Every time the clouds drop in rain, every time the waters freeze into new ice, every time the juices of nature gather into another violet, every time a new wail of life is heard upon a mother's breast, every time you breathe another sigh, or shed another tear, there is God as truly present in His miraculous creative capacity as on the day when He said 'Let there be light'. *The author of this passage, P. S. Menzies, was a little-known Victorian minister in Australia who died aged only 34.*

<u>SEPTEMBER 4</u>

I mourn not that my lot is low;
I wish no higher state.
I sigh not that fate made me so,
Nor tease her to be great.
I am content, for well I see
What all at last shall find,
That life's worst lot the best shall be,
And that's a quiet mind.

JOHN CLARE

SEPTEMBER

Love or friendship for ourselves does exist. With a soul at unity in itself, the man will be his own friend. But such friendship for self will exist only in the good man; for in him alone the parts of the soul being nowise at variance, are well disposed towards one another. For the bad man, being ever at strife with himself, can never be his own friend, *wrote Aristotle more than two thousand years ago. He perceived what modern psychologists often fail to see – that we can only love ourselves if our behaviour is worth loving.*

SEPTEMBER 5

Lives of great men all remind us,
We can make our lives sublime,
And, departing, leave behind us,
Footprints on the sands of time; –

Footprints, that perhaps another,
Sailing o'er life's solemn main,
A forlorn and shipwrecked brother,
Seeing, shall take heart again.

HENRY WADSWORTH LONGFELLOW

SEPTEMBER 6

Have you noticed how the pebbles of the road are polished and pure after the rain? And the flowers? No word can describe them. One can only murmur an 'Ah' of admiration. A Japanese writer and bonze has said that one should understand the 'Ah' of things.

A MASTER OF ZEN BUDDHISM

SEPTEMBER 7

SEPTEMBER 8   Tomorrow makes today's whole head sick, its whole heart faint. When we should be still, sleeping or dreaming, we are fretting about an hour that lies a half sun's journey away! Not so doest thou, Lord.

GEORGE MACDONALD

SEPTEMBER 9

Earth's crammed with heaven
And every common bush afire with God;
But only he who sees, takes off his shoes, –
The rest sit round it and pluck blackberries.

ELIZABETH BARRETT BROWNING

SEPTEMBER 10   Among some distressful emergencies that I have experienced in life, I ever laid this down as my foundation of comfort – that he who has lived the life of an honest man has by no means lived in vain!

This comforting passage comes from a letter written by Robert Burns to a friend in misfortune.

SEPTEMBER 11

Do all the good you can,
By all the means you can,
In all the ways you can,
In all the places you can,
To all the people you can.
As long as ever you can.

I like the simplicity of this verse by John Wesley, the founder of Methodism. It's a good guide to a good life.

SEPTEMBER

A pebble in the streamlet scant
Has turned the course of many a river;
A dewdrop in the baby plant
Has warped the giant oak for ever

AUTHOR UNKNOWN

SEPTEMBER 12

There is an inscription in one of the churches in the City of London, which tells the story of a mother cat and her kitten during the bombing of the Second World War. On Monday, September 9th, 1940, she endured horrors and perils beyond the power of words to tell. Shielding her kitten in a sort of recess in the house (a spot she selected only three days before the tragedies occurred), she sat the whole frightful night of bombing and fire, guarding her little kitten. The roofs and masonry exploded, the whole house blazed, four floors fell through in front of her. Fire and ruin all around her. Yet she stayed calm and steadfast and waited for help. We rescued her in the early morning while the place was still burning, and by the mercy of Almighty God she and her kitten were not only saved but unhurt.

SEPTEMBER 13

SEPTEMBER 14

When I sit by myself at the close of the day,
And watch the blue twilight turn amber and grey,
With fancies as twinkling and vague as the stars,
And as distant as they from this life's petty jars –
I know not, I think not where fortune may be,
But I feel I am in very good company.

When I sit with a friend at the glow of the hearth,
And fight some great battle of wisdom or mirth,
And strike from our armour the sparkle of wit,
That follows the shafts of our thoughts when they hit.
I know not, I think not where fortune may be,
But I feel I am in very good company.

GLOUCESTERSHIRE FOLKSONG

SEPTEMBER 15

Edward Wilson accompanied Captain Scott on his Antarctic expeditions. In his diaries he wrote:

In refusing to be put out and annoyed, you are taking God's hand in yours. And once you feel God's hand, or the hand of anyone that loves good, in yours, let pity take the place of irritation, let silence take the place of a hasty answer.

SEPTEMBER

Love seeketh not itself to please
Nor for itself hath any care,
But for another gives its ease
And builds a heaven in hell's despair.

WILLIAM BLAKE

A famous Jewish scholar, rabbi Zusya, said to his followers just before his death:

In the world to come I shall not be asked: 'Why were you not Moses?' But God will ask me 'Why were you not Zusya?'

Oh why is heaven built so far,
Oh why is earth set so remote?
I cannot reach the nearest star
That hangs afloat.

For I am bound with fleshly bands,
Joy, beauty, lie beyond my scope;
I strain my heart, I stretch my hands,
And catch at hope.

CHRISTINA ROSSETTI

For we can do nothing of ourselves; but being called, being drawn, being required to do that which is far beyond our strength, and giving up thereto; the life springs, the power appears, which does the work.

God gives us the power we need, says Isaac Penington.

SEPTEMBER 20

To walk staunchly by the best light one has, to be strict and sincere with oneself, not to be of the number of those who say and do not, to be in earnest, – this is the discipline by which alone man is enabled to rescue his life from thraldom to the passing moment and to his bodily senses, to ennoble it, and make it eternal.

MATTHEW ARNOLD

SEPTEMBER 21

Thrice happy, who free from ambition and pride,
In a rural retreat, has a quiet fireside;
I love my fireside, there I long to repair,
And to drink a delightful oblivion of care.

Poets rarely write about the cosiness of home, so these lines by Isaac Hawkins Browne are unusual ones.

SEPTEMBER 22

Good example is a language and an argument which everybody understands.

BISHOP THOMAS WILSON

SEPTEMBER 23

No longer forward nor behind
I look in hope or fear,
But grateful, take the good I find,
The best of now and here.

The secret of happiness seems to be to live in the present, rather than fear the future or regret the past – the theme of John Greenleaf Whittier's verse.

SEPTEMBER

Love is indeed heaven upon earth; since heaven above would not be heaven without it. What we love we will hear; what we love, we will trust; and what we love, we will serve, aye, and suffer for too.

WILLIAM PENN

Our birth is but a sleep and a forgetting;
The Soul that rises with us, our life's star
Hath had elsewhere its setting,
And cometh from afar;
Not in entire forgetfulness,
And not in utter nakedness,
But trailing clouds of glory do we come
From God, who is our home:
Heaven lies about us in our infancy;
Shades of the prison-house begin to close
Upon the growing boy,
But he beholds the light, and whence it flows,
He sees it in his joy.

William Wordsworth's beautiful verse describes how children have a vision of life that adults have lost.

SEPTEMBER

SEPTEMBER 26   I think I could turn and live with animals, they are so placid
and self-contained.
I stand and look at them long and long.
They do not sweat and whine about their condition,
They do not lie awake in the dark and weep for their sins,
They do not make me sick discussing their duty to God,
Not one is dissatisfied, not one is demented with the mania of
owning things,
Not one kneels to another, nor to his kind that lived thousands
of years ago,
Not one is respectable or unhappy over the whole earth.

WALT WHITMAN

SEPTEMBER 27   One is happy as a result of one's own efforts, once one knows
the necessary ingredients of happiness – simple tastes, a
certain degree of courage, self-denial to a point, love of work,
and above all, a clear conscience. Happiness is no vague
dream.

GEORGE SAND

SEPTEMBER

Men's proper business in this world falls mainly into three divisions: –

First to know ourselves, and the existing state of the things they have to do with.

Secondly, to be happy in themselves, and in the existing state of things.

Thirdly, to mend themselves, and the existing state of things, as far as either are marred and mendable.

Sometimes, particularly when I am downcast, I wonder why we are here on earth. The Victorian thinker, John Ruskin, gave this thoughtful answer.

SEPTEMBER 28

O man! hold thee on in courage of soul
Through the stormy shades of thy worldly way,
And the billows of cloud that around thee roll
Shall sleep in the light of a wondrous day.

PERCY BYSSHE SHELLEY

SEPTEMBER 29

O Lord, remember not only the men and women of good will, but also those of ill will. But do not remember all the suffering they have inflicted on us; remember the fruits we have bought, thanks to this suffering – our comradeship, our loyalty, our humility, our courage, our generosity, the greatness of heart which has grown out of all this, and when they come to judgement let all the fruits which we have borne be their forgiveness. *This prayer was written by an unknown prisoner in Ravensbruck concentration camp.*

SEPTEMBER 30

OCTOBER

Epictetus was a Stoic philosopher living in the times of the Romans. He suggested some rules for living which are still useful today. I will give you a few rules for everyday life. Whatever you are doing do it with all your might. Do not let your behaviour and manners vary according to the station in life of the person you are dealing with – a servant is as much entitled to politeness as Caesar is. Always behave quietly, imperturbably and with decorum. Try to feel pleasure and not envy at other people's successes. Let motives mean more to you than results.

Very few plays and poems are about ordinary working folk. Thomas Dekker, an Elizabethan playwright, wrote The Shoemaker's Holiday, a play all about merry cobblers and their apprentices. They sing this song.

> Art thou poor, yet hast thou golden
> slumbers?
> O, sweet content!
> Art thou rich, yet is thy mind perplexed?
> O, punishment!
> Dost thou laugh to see how fools are vexed
> To add to golden numbers golden numbers?
> O, sweet content. O, sweet content.
> Work apace, apace, apace, apace;
> Honest labour bears a lovely face.

OCTOBER 3

Be still, sad heart! and cease repining;
Behind the clouds is the sun still shining;
Thy fate is the common fate of all,
Into each life some rain must fall.

HENRY WADSWORTH LONGFELLOW

OCTOBER 4

Today is the feast day of St Francis of Assisi, and this is his prayer, one of the noblest ever uttered.

Lord, make me a channel of thy peace; that where there is hatred, I may bring love; that where there is wrong, I may bring the spirit of forgiveness; that where there is discord, I may bring harmony; that where there is error, I may bring truth; that where there is doubt, I may bring faith; that where there is despair, I may bring hope; that where there are shadows, I may bring light; that where there is sadness, I may bring joy. Lord, grant that I may seek rather to comfort than to be comforted; to understand rather than to be understood; to love, rather than to be loved. For it is by self-forgetting that one finds. It is by forgiving that one is forgiven.

OCTOBER

We may promote the happiness of those with whom He has placed us in society, by acting honestly towards all, benevolently to those who fall within our way, respecting sacredly their rights, bodily and mental, and cherishing especially their freedom of conscience.

THOMAS JEFFERSON

Where art thou beloved Tomorrow?
When young and old, strong and weak,
Rich and poor, through joy and sorrow,
They sweet smiles we ever seek.
In thy place – ah well-a-day! –
We find the thing we fled – Today.

Happiness lies in living in the day, rather than looking forward to the future or backwards to the past. Percy Bysshe Shelley reminds us with this poignant verse.

Have mercy on me, O Beneficent One, I was angered for I had no shoes: then I met a man who had no feet.

CHINESE SAYING

The world is a mirror of infinite beauty, yet no man sees it. It is the temple of majesty yet no man regards it. It is a region of light and peace, did not men disquiet it. It is the paradise of God, *wrote Thomas Traherne, a seventeenth-century mystic, who believed that this world showed us the beauty of God.*

OCTOBER 9

O man, forgive thy mortal foe,
Nor ever strike him blow for blow;
For all the souls on earth that live,
To be forgiven must forgive;
Forgive him seventy times and seven,
For all the blessed souls in heaven
Are both forgivers and forgiven.

This verse is found on a gravestone in a New York cemetery. Amongst those I must forgive is myself for if God can forgive me, I surely must forgive myself.

OCTOBER 10   Everything that is done in the world is done by hope.

MARTIN LUTHER

OCTOBER 11

I held it truth, with him who sings
To one clear harp in diverse tones,
That men may rise on stepping stones
Of their dead selves to higher things,

For me these lines by Alfred Tennyson are among the most inspiring of all the poetry I have ever read. Most of us fall short of what we would like to be but we use our mistakes and our sins as steps to a new life.

OCTOBER 12   A man's life of each day depends for its solidity and value on whether he reads during that day and, far more still, on what he reads during it.

MATTHEW ARNOLD

OCTOBER

The country life is to be preferred, for there we see the works of God; but in cities, little else but the works of men: and the one makes a better subject for our contemplation than the other.

WILLIAM PENN

We can find inspiration in the common things of life. The poet, Algernon Swinburne, found it in babies.

A baby's feet, like sea shells pink,
Might tempt, should heaven see meet,
An angel's lips to kiss, we think,
A baby's feet.

Like rose-hued sea-flowers toward the heat
They stretch and spread and wink
Their ten soft buds that part and meet.

No flower-bells that expand and shrink
Gleam half so heavenly sweet,
As shine on life's untrodden brink
A baby's feet.

OCTOBER 15   Life is to be fortified by many friendships. To love and to be loved, is the greatest happiness of existence. I could and would not live if I were alone upon the earth, and cut off from the remembrance of my fellow-creatures. It is not that a man has occasion often to fall back upon the kindness of his friends; perhaps he may never experience the necessity of doing so; but they stand there as a solid and impregnable bulwark against all the evils of life.

SYDNEY SMITH

OCTOBER 16

Sweet little bird in russet coat
The livery of the closing year
I love thy lonely plaintive note
And tiny whispering song to hear.
While on the style or garden seat
I sit to watch the falling leaves
The songs thy little joys repeat
My loneliness relieves.

The robin sings when other birds are silent. Like John Clare, I feel its song is somehow comforting.

OCTOBER

Love is swift, pure, meek, joyous and glad, strong, patient, faithful, wise, forbearing, manly, and never seeketh himself or his own will; for whensoever a man seeketh himself, he falleth from love. Also love is circumspect, meek, righteous; not tender, not light, nor heeding vain things; sober, chaste, stable, quiet, and well stabled in his outward wits . . . Without some sorrow or pain no man may live in love.

THOMAS À KEMPIS

St Luke's little summer starts this day. From a seventeenth-century writer, Francis Pastorius of Pennsylvania, comes this verse for a sundial:

Keep in God's way; keep pace with every hour;
Hurt none; do all the good that's in your power.
Hours can't look back at all; they'll stay for none;
Treat sure, keep up with them, and all's your own.

Self love, my liege, is not so vile a sin as self neglecting, *wrote William Shakespeare.*

If the doors of perception were cleansed, everything would appear to man as it is, infinite.
For man has closed himself up, till he sees all things through narrow chinks of his cavern.

I feel I understand these mystical lines by the poet William Blake but I doubt if I could explain them.

OCTOBER 21 Hope is itself a species of happiness, and perhaps, the chief happiness which this world affords.

ANONYMOUS

OCTOBER 22

Take time to THINK . . .
it is the source of power.
Take time to PLAY . . .
it is the secret of perpetual youth.
Take time to READ . . .
it is the fountain of wisdom.
Take time to PRAY . . .
it is the greatest power on earth.
Take time to LAUGH . . .
it is the music of the soul.
Take time to GIVE . . .
it is too short a day to be selfish.

AUTHOR UNKNOWN

OCTOBER 23 I must first know myself. To be curious about that which is not my concern, while I am still in ignorance of my own self, would be ridiculous, *said the Greek philosopher, Socrates. Another saying attributed to him is:* The unexamined life is not worth living.

OCTOBER 24 *The great composer Ludwig von Beethoven was inspired by the beauty of woods and trees. At this time of year the autumn colours make them beautiful.*

Almighty One, in the woods I am blessed. Happy everyone in the woods. Every tree speaks through thee. O God! What glory in the woodland! On the heights is peace – peace to serve Him.

A man who cannot find tranquillity within himself will search for it in vain elsewhere.

DUC DE LA ROCHEFOUCAULD

These I have loved:
White plates and cups, clean-gleaming,
Ringed with blue lines; and feathery faery dust;
Wet roofs, beneath the lamp-light; the strong crust
Of friendly bread; and many-tasting food;
Rainbows and the blue bitter smoke of wood;
And radiant raindrops couching in cool flowers;
And flowers themselves, that sway through sunny hours,
Dreaming of moths that drink them under the moon;
Then, the cool kindliness of sheets, that soon
Smooth away trouble . . .

RUPERT BROOKE

OCTOBER 27   *Thomas Hardy wrote this poem about the last chrysanthemum which continues flowering through the frost of approaching winter.*

> Too late its beauty, lonely thing,
> The season's shine is spent,
> Nothing remains for it but shivering
> In tempests turbulent.
>
> Had it a reason for delay,
> Dreaming in witlessness
> That for a bloom so delicately gay
> Winter would stay its stress?
>
> I talk as if the thing were born
> With sense to work its mind;
> Yet it is but one mask of many worn
> By the Great Face behind.

OCTOBER 28   One grain of time's inestimable sand is worth a golden mountain: let us not lose it, *wrote Roger Williams, the seventeenth-century founder of Providence, in New England.*

OCTOBER

The variety of forms in the world is the beauty of the world, *wrote* *William Dell,* *a* *seventeenth-century* *preacher* *who* *argued* *passionately* *in* *favour* *of* *the* *individual's* *right* *to* *follow* *his* *own* *conscience.*

OCTOBER 29

And could you keep your heart in wonder at the daily miracles of life, your pain would not seem less wondrous than your joy, *wrote the Lebanese poet and philosopher, Kahlil Gibran.*

OCTOBER 30

They are all gone into the world of light!
And I alone sit lingering here;
Their very memory is fair and bright,
And my sad thoughts doth clear.

I see them walking in an air of glory,
Whose lights doth trample on my days:
My days, which are at best but dull and hoary,
Mere glimmerings and decays.

And yet as angels in some brighter dreams
Call to the soul, when man doth sleep:
So some strange thoughts transcend our wonted themes,
And into glory peep.

OCTOBER 31

For Halloween what could be better than this moving poem about friends who have died by Henry Vaughan, best known for his hymm My Soul There is a Country.

NOVEMBER

NOVEMBER 1

There is still beauty in the dying months of the year, as this sonnet by John Clare reminds us.

Now that the year is drawing to a close,
Such mellow tints on trees and bushes lie
So like to sunshine, that it brighter glows
As one looks more intently, – on the sky
I turn astonished that no sun is there.
The ribboned strips of orange, blue and red
Streak through the western sky, a gorgeous bed,
Painting day's end most beautifully fair.
So mild, so quiet breathes the balmy air
Scenting the perfume of decaying leaves,
Such fragrance and such loveliness they wear –
Trees, hedgerows, bushes – that the heart receives
Joy for which language owneth words too few
To paint that glowing richness which I view.

NOVEMBER 2

Nowhere can a man find greater or a more untroubled retreat than in his own soul; above all, he who possesses resources in himself, which he need only contemplate to secure immediate ease of mind – the ease which is but another word for a well-ordered spirit. Avail yourself often, then, of this retirement, and so continually renew yourself.

MARCUS AURELIUS

NOVEMBER

NOVEMBER 3   *In the darkest days of the year, there is still inspiration to be found in the rain and frost and sleet. This verse by Henry Vaughan shows the way.*

> When seasons change, then lay before thine eyes
> His wondrous method; mark the various scenes
> In heaven; hail, thunder, rainbows, snow and ice,
> Calms, tempests, light and darkness by His means;
> Thou canst not miss His praise; each tree, herb, flower
> Are shadows of His wisdom and His power.

NOVEMBER 4   For if a man strikes many coins from the one mould, they all resemble one another; but the supreme King of Kings, the Holy One, blessed be He, fashioned every man in the stamp of the first man, and yet not one of them resembles his fellows. Therefore every single person is obliged to say: 'The world was created for my sake.' *This inspiring passage comes from the Talmud, the holy scriptures of the Jews. I can't have a bad day if I wake up thinking the world was created specially for me and I was created specially for it.*

NOVEMBER

Do not linger with regretting,
Or for passing hours despond;
Nor, the daily toil forgetting,
Look too eagerly beyond.

Adelaide Proctor, the author of this verse, was well known for her poems a hundred years ago.

The sayings of Lao-Tzu, a Chinese philosopher living in the sixth century after Christ, were written down by his followers. Here is one of them. I have three precious things, which I hold fast and prize. The first is gentleness; the second is frugality; the third is humility, which keeps me from putting myself before others. Be gentle and you can be bold; be frugal and you can be liberal; avoid putting yourself before others and you can become a leader among men.

John Greenleaf Whittier's poem celebrates the unexpectedly warm days of the late autumn.

The summer and the winter here
Midway a truce are holding,
A soft, consenting atmosphere
Their tents of peace enfolding.

Old cares grow light; aside I lay
The doubts and fears that troubled;
The quiet of the happy day
Within my soul is doubled.

NOVEMBER 8   *We lead such busy lives in the modern world I like to remember the advice of the Quaker William Penn:*

In the rush and noise of life, as you have intervals, step home within yourselves and be still. Wait upon God, and feel his good presence; this will carry you evenly through your day's business.

NOVEMBER 9

The bright moon shining overhead,
The stream beneath the breeze's touch,
Are pure and perfect joys indeed, –
But few are they who think them such.

ANONYMOUS CHINESE POET

NOVEMBER 10

Do your duty and leave the rest to Providence.

STONEWALL JACKSON

NOVEMBER 11   *On the eleventh hour of the eleventh day of the eleventh month, peace was signed, ending the First World War. It is not fashionable to be patriotic, but most people love their country, as well as their family, friends and home, as Thomas Campbell writes:*

Breathes there the man with soul so dead,
Who never to himself hath said,
'This is my own, my native land!'
Whose heart hath ne'er within him burned
As home his footsteps he hath turned
From wandering on a foreign strand.

NOVEMBER

Though you cannot see, when you take one step, what will be the next, yet follow truth, justice and plain dealing, and never fear their leading you out of the labyrinth, in the easiest manner possible. The knot which you thought a Gordian one, will untie itself before you. Nothing is so mistaken as the supposition, that a person is to extricate himself from a difficulty, by intrigue, by an untruth, by an injustice. *This advice, from Thomas Jefferson, needs courage.*

The most gentle of all poets, William Cowper, lived a quiet life in the country, devoted to his home, his garden and his pets. Other poets have written about love, romance and passion: Cowper celebrated the cosy domestic pleasures of an ordinary life.

> Now stir the fire, and close the shutters fast,
> Let fall the curtains, wheel the sofa round,
> And while the bubbling and loud-hissing urn
> Throws up a steamy column, and the cups,
> That cheer but not inebriate, wait on each,
> So let us welcome peaceful evening in.

To be honest;
to be kind;
to earn a little
and to spend a little less;
to make, upon the whole,
a family happier for his presence;
to renounce, when that shall be necessary,
and not be embittered;
to keep a few friends,
but these without capitulation;
above all, in the same condition,
to keep friends with himself;
here is a task for all that a man has of fortitude and
     delicacy.

ROBERT LOUIS STEVENSON

How do you know but every bird that cuts the airy way
Is an immense world of delight, closed by your senses five?

WILLIAM BLAKE

NOVEMBER

The smallest particle of good realised and applied to life, a NOVEMBER 16 single vivid experience of love, will advance us much farther, will far more surely protect our soul from evil, than the most arduous struggle against sin.

FATHER ELCHANINOV

Dorothy Wordsdworth, sister of the poet William, could see beauty NOVEMBER 17 *even in the way the November winds hurl down the leaves. She wrote in her diary:* What a beautiful thing God has made winter to be by stripping the trees and letting us see their shapes and forms. What a freedom does it seem to give to the storms

To let go is not to judge – NOVEMBER 18
But to allow another to be a human being.
To let go is not to try to change or blame another –
It is to make the most of myself.

AUTHOR UNKNOWN

St Godric was a Celtic saint who loved animals. The gentleness of NOVEMBER 19 his heart did not betray itself only in kindness to men, but his wise solicitude watched over the very reptiles and creatures of the earth. For in winter when all about was frozen stiff in the cold, he would go out barefoot, and if he lighted on any animal helpless with misery of the cold, he would set it under his armpit or in his bosom to warm it.

NOVEMBER 20

Then, welcome each rebuff
That turns earth's smoothness rough,
Each sting that bids nor sit nor stand but go!
Be our joys three-parts pain!
Strive, and hold cheap the strain;
Learn, nor account the pang; dare, never grudge the
throe!

Try to see, with the poet Robert Browning, that life's difficulties are opportunities not unfair punishments.

NOVEMBER 21

Be not afraid of life. Believe that life is worth living, and your belief will help create the fact.

WILLIAM JAMES

NOVEMBER 22

Today is St Cecilia's day, the patron saint of music – a day to recall the lines of Alexander Pope, the eighteenth-century poet, about the power of music.

Music the fiercest grief can charm,
And fate's severest rage disarm:
Music can soften pain to ease,
And make despair and madness please;
Our joys below it can improve,
And antedate the bliss above.

NOVEMBER 23

Kindness is a language which the blind can see and the deaf can hear.

AUTHOR UNKNOWN

NOVEMBER

Blessed are those who listen, for they shall learn.

AUTHOR UNKNOWN

The poet Thomas Hardy wrote these verses on a gloomy winter day
hearing a thrush's song.

At once a voice arose among
The bleak twigs overhead
In a full-hearted evensong
Of joy illimited;
An aged thrush, frail, gaunt and small,
In blast-beruffled plume,
Had chosen thus to fling his soul
Upon the growing gloom.

So little cause for carolings
Of such ecstatic sound
Was written on terrestrial things
Afar or nigh around,
That I could think there trembled through
His happy good-night air
Some blessed Hope, whereof he knew
And I was unaware.

NOVEMBER 26

Forth in thy name, O Lord, I go,
My daily labour to pursue;
Thee, only thee, resolved to know,
In all I think, or speak, or do.

The task thy wisdom hath assigned
O let me cheerfully fulfil:
In all my works thy presence find,
And prove thine acceptable will.

CHARLES WESLEY

NOVEMBER 27

All that is sweet, delightful and amiable in this world, in the serenity of the air, the fineness of the seasons, the joy of light, the melody of sounds, the beauty of colours, the fragrancy of smells, the splendour of precious stones, is nothing else but Heaven breaking through the veil of this world, manifesting itself in such a degree and darting forth in such variety so much of its own nature. *This wonderful passage comes from William Law, a clergyman who lived a simple, faithful and holy life.*

Doing an injury puts you below your enemy;
Revenging one makes you but even with him;
Forgiving it sets you above him.

BENJAMIN FRANKLIN

Just for today I will try to live through this day only, and not tackle my whole life problem at once. I can do something for twelve hours that would appal me if I felt that I had to keep it up for a lifetime.
Just for today I will be happy. Most folks are as happy as they make up their minds to be.
Just for today I will adjust myself to what is and not try to adjust everything to my own desires. I will take my luck as it comes and fit myself to it.
Just for today I will have a quiet half hour all by myself and relax. During this half hour, sometime, I will try to get a better perspective of my life.
   Just for today I will be unafraid. Especially I will not be afraid to enjoy what is beautiful, and to believe that as I give to the world, so the world will give to me. *A friend who belongs to Alcoholics Anonymous gave me a card with this message on it. It helps him stay sober. It helps me stay happy.*

Nobody is truly a Christian unless his cat or dog is the better off for it.

ROWLAND HILL

DECEMBER

On frosty December nights, I look up at the stars and think of my favourite hymn written by Joseph Addison.

> The spacious firmament on high,
> With all the blue ethereal sky,
> And spangled heavens, a shining frame,
> Their great Original proclaim:
> The unwearied sun, from day to day,
> Does his Creator's power display,
> And publishes to every land,
> The work of an Almighty hand.
>
> Soon as the evening shades prevail,
> The moon takes up the wondrous tale,
> And nightly to the listening earth
> Repeats the story of her birth:
> Whilst all the stars that round her burn,
> And all the planets, in their turn,
> Confirm the tidings as they roll,
> And spread the truth from pole to pole.

Courage is reckoned the greatest of all virtues, because, unless a man has that virtue, he has no security for preserving any other, *said the eighteenth-century writer Dr Samuel Johnson. It takes courage to hold on to our ideals and to put them into practice.*

DECEMBER

DECEMBER 3   *At the end of the year, the days are closing in, the blood seems to run thin with cold and I feel tired and downhearted,. These verses by the Victorian poet Arthur Hugh Clough reassure me that all is well.*

Say not the struggle nought availeth
The labour and the wounds are vain,
The enemy faints not, nor faileth,
And as things have been they remain.

If hopes were dupes, fears may be liars;
It may be in yon smoke concealed,
Your comrades chase e'en now the fliers,
And, but for you, possess the field.

For while the tired waves, vainly breaking,
Seem here no painful inch to gain,
Far back, through creeks and inlets making,
Comes silent, flooding in, the main.

And not by eastern windows only,
When daylight comes, comes in the light;
In front the sun climbs slow, how slowly!
But westward, look, the land is bright!

DECEMBER

Let us not be satisfied with just giving money. Money is not enough, money can be got, but they need your hearts to love them. So, spread love everywhere you go: first of all in your own home. Give love to your children, to your wife or husband, to a next-door neighbour. *A saying of Mother Teresa of Calcutta.*

DECEMBER 4

I am so fond of books that I treasure these lines by the eighteenth-century poet, George Crabbe.

DECEMBER 5

> But what strange art, what magic can dispose
> The troubled mind to change its native woes?
> This, books can do – nor this alone: they give
> New views to life and teach us how to live;
> Their aid they yield to all: they never shun
> The man of sorrow or the wretch undone.

At the judgement day a man will be called to account for all the good things he might have enjoyed and did not enjoy – *a Jewish proverb with much wisdom in it.*

DECEMBER 6

> A thing of beauty is a joy for ever:
> Its loveliness increases; it will never
> Pass into nothingness; but still will keep
> A bower quiet for us, and a sleep
> Full of sweet dreams, and health, and quiet breathing.

DECEMBER 7

These lines about beauty by the poet John Keats cannot fail to inspire anybody who has eyes to see.

DECEMBER

DECEMBER 8   Look thou be not curious in searching of any other man's life, neither do thou busy thyself with those things which do not belong unto thee. What is it to thee whether this man be good or bad; whether he say or do this or that? Thou needest not to answer for another man's deeds, but for thine own thou must needly answer.

THOMAS À KEMPIS

DECEMBER 9   *The American poet, Henry Wadsworth Longfellow, called this poem Santa Teresa's Book-Mark. What a lovely inscription for a bookmark it is.*

> Let nothing disturb thee;
> Nothing affright thee;
> All things are passing;
> God never changeth;
> Patient endurance
> Attaineth to all things;
> Who God possesseth
> In nothing is wanting;
> Alone God sufficeth.

DECEMBER 10   Whatsoever things are true, whatsoever things are honest, whatsoever things are just, whatsoever things are pure, whatsoever things are lovely, whatsoever things are of good repute, if there be any virtue, and if there be any praise, think on these things.

ST PAUL'S EPISTLE TO THE PHILIPPIANS

DECEMBER

The cold weather often makes me appreciate the warmth and comfort indoors. Christina Rossetti's poem makes me thankful for home comforts. I think we often undervalue the pleasure of cosiness ... something that this poem conveys quite strongly.

Sweet blackbird is silenced with chaffinch and thrush,
Only waistcoated robin still chirps in the bush:
Soft sun-loving swallows have mustered in force,
And winged to the spice-teeming southlands their course.

Plump housekeeper dormouse has tucked himself neat,
Just a brown ball in moss with a morsel to eat:
Armed hedgehog has huddled him into the hedge,
While frogs scarce miss freezing deep down in the sedge.

Soft swallows have left us alone in the lurch,
But robin sits whistling to us from his perch:
If I were red robin, I'd pipe you a tune
Would make you despise all the beauties of June.

But, since that cannot be, let us draw round the fire,
Munch chestnuts, tell stories, and stir the blaze higher.

DECEMBER 12

Jog on, jog on, the footpath way,
And merrily hent the stile-a:
A merry heart goes all the day,
And your sad heart tires in a mile-a

Your paltry money-bags of gold,
What need have we to stare for?
When little or nothing soon is told,
And we have the less to care for.

TRADITIONAL BALLAD

DECEMBER 13

The explorer of the Antarctic Captain Robert Scott spent his last hours alive, writing a farewell letter. It is a testament to cheerfulness in the worst kind of adversity and a written proof of courage. Goodbye – I am not at all afraid of the end, but sad to miss many a simple pleasure which I had planned for the future in our long marches . . . We are in a desperate state – feet frozen, etc., no fuel, and a long way from food, but it would do your heart good to be in our tent, to hear our songs and our cheery conversation.

DECEMBER

Life is a precious and unique gift, and we squander it foolishly and carelessly, forgetful of its brevity. Either we look back with yearning on the past or else we live in the expectation of a future in which, it seems to us, life will really begin; whereas the present – that is, our life as it actually is – is wasted in these fruitless dreams and regrets.

DECEMBER 14

FATHER ELCHANINOV

So in those winters of the soul,
By bitter blasts and drear
O'erswept from memory's frozen pole,
Will sunny days appear,
Reviving hope and faith, they show
The soul its living powers,
And how beneath the winter's snow
Lie germs of summer flowers!

DECEMBER 15

This verse from John Greenleaf Whittier never fails to cheer me up. The worst days have some good in them, and after all we can start the day afresh at any time.

Humour is the great thing, the saving thing, after all. The minute it crops up, all our hardnesses yield, all our irritations and resentments flit away, and a sunny spirit takes their place. The best way to cheer yourself is to try to cheer somebody else up, *said Mark Twain. He was a man who practised what he preached: his jokes were usually funny without being malicious.*

DECEMBER 16

DECEMBER 17   May I be no man's enemy, and may I be the friend of that
which is eternal and abides.
May I never quarrel with those nearest to me: and if I do, may
I be reconciled quickly.
May I love, seek, and attain only that which is good.
May I wish for all men's happiness and envy none.
May I never rejoice in the ill fortune of one who has
wronged me.
May I win no victory that harms either me or my opponent.

This prayer is by Eusebius, a Platonist philosopher.

DECEMBER 18   *Now's the time for gathering friends and families together. Three
hundred years ago Nicholas Breton wrote:* It is a holy time, a duty
in Christians, for the remembrance of Christ, and custom
among friends for the maintenance of good fellowship. I hold
it a memory of Heaven's love, and the world's peace, the
mirth of the honest and the meeting of the friendly.

DECEMBER 19   Christmas comes
Ushered with a rain of plums;
Hollies in the windows greet him,
Schools come driving home to meet him;
Every mouth delights to name him;
Wet and cold, and winds and dark,
Mark him but the warmer mark.

LEIGH HUNT

DECEMBER

I love this strange carol written 500 years ago.

There is no rose of such virtue
As is the rose that bear Jesu
　　　　Alleluia.

For in this rose contained was
Heaven and earth in little space
　　　　Res miranda.

By that rose we may well see
There be one God in persons three
　　　　Pares forma.

It is in the old Christmas carols, that we find not only what makes Christmas poetic and soothing and stately, but first and foremost what makes Christmas exciting. The exciting quality of Christmas rests upon an ancient paradox. It rests upon the great paradox that the power and centre of the whole universe may be found in some seemingly small matter, that the stars in their courses may move like a moving wheel round the neglected outhouse of an inn.

G. K. CHESTERTON

DECEMBER 22 In everyone there is something precious, found in no one else; so honour each man for what is hidden within him – for what he alone has, and none of his fellows.

HASIDIC SAYING

DECEMBER 23 I salute you. There is nothing I can give you which you have not; but there is much that, while I cannot give you, you can take.

No heaven can come to us unless our hearts find rest in it today:

Take heaven.

No peace lies in the future which is not hidden in the present:

Take peace.

The gloom of the world is but a shadow; behind it, yet within our reach is joy:

Take joy.

And so at this Christmas time I greet you, with the prayer that for you, now and forever, the day breaks and the shadows flee away.

FRA GIOVANNI

DECEMBER

Now thrice welcome Christmas
Which brings us good cheer,
Minced pies and plum porridge,
Good ale and strong beer;
With pig, goose and capon,
The best that may be,
So well doth the weather
And our stomachs agree.

ANON

In the beginning was the Word, and the Word was with God, and the Word was God. The same was in the beginning with God. All things were made by him; and without him was not any thing made. In him was life: and the life was the light of men. And the light shineth in darkness; and the darkness comprehended it not . . . That was the true Light, which lighteth every man that cometh into the world.

ST JOHN'S GOSPEL

The Victorian poet Charles Mackay wrote about making up old quarrels at Christmas under the holly.

Let sinned-against and sinning
Forget their strife's beginning,
And join in friendship now,
Be links no longer broken,
Be sweet forgiveness spoken
Under the holly bough.

DECEMBER

DECEMBER 27 There may be degrees of glory but not of happiness.
One star differeth from another in glory, but both are stars,
and both bright according to their bulk. *Bishop Thomas Wilson's
words remind me not to compare myself with others, usually to my
own pain or envy.*

DECEMBER 28 The tree which moves some to tears of joy is, in the eye of
others, only a green thing which stands in the way. As a man
is, so he sees.

WILLIAM BLAKE

DECEMBER 29 Neither in thy actions be sluggish, nor in thy conversation
without method, nor wandering in thy thoughts, nor let there
be in thy soul inward contention, nor in life be so busy as to
have no leisure.

MARCUS AURELIUS

DECEMBER 30 *The birth date of Rudyard Kipling seems a good day for what I think
are the best lines of his famous poem, If.*

If you can dream – and not make dreams your master
If you can think – and not make thoughts your aim
If you can meet with Triumph and Disaster
And treat those two imposters as the same . . .
If you can fill the unforgiving minute
With sixty seconds' worth of distance run,
Yours is the Earth and everything that's in it,
And – which is more – you'll be a Man, my son!

DECEMBER

There is a great solemnity about the end of the year but it is a time not to look back with regret, but to try to look forward with hope and trust. Alfred Tennyson's poem In Memoriam *sums this up for me.*

Ring out, wild bells, to the wild sky,
　　The flying cloud, the frosty light:
　　The year is dying in the night;
Ring out, wild bells, and let him die.

Ring out the old, ring in the new,
　　Ring, happy bells, across the snow:
　　The year is going, let him go;
Ring out the false, ring in the true.

Ring out the grief that saps the mind,
　　For those that here we see no more;
　　Ring out the feud of rich and poor,
Ring in redress to all mankind.

Ring in the valiant man and free,
　　The larger heart, the kindlier hand;
　　Ring out the darkness of the land,
Ring in the Christ that is to be.

ACKNOWLEDGEMENTS

For permission to reproduce copyright material in this book, the author and publisher gratefully acknowledge the following:

C. S. Lewis, *Mere Christianity*, Collins Fount; Mother Teresa of Calcutta, *A Gift from God*. Collins Fount; David Higham Associates Ltd for permission to quote from *Gazing On*; Kitty Muggeridge, *Truth*, SPCK; George Appleton, The prayer for animals, *One Man's Prayers*, SPCK; *London*, © George Appleton, 1967; Khalil Gibran, *The Prophet*, Alfred A. Knopf, New York; Orin L. Crain, *Slow Me Down, Lord*, The Open Church Foundation, at P.O. Box 81389-0004, Wellesley Hills, MA 02181, USA; Robert Lynd, an extract from an essay, exact origin unknown, J.M. Dent and Sons Ltd; Paul Tillich, *The Shaking of the Foundations*, SCM Press Ltd, London, and Charles Scribner's Sons, an imprint of Macmillan Publishing Company, New York. Copyright 1948 Charles Scribner's Sons; copyright renewed 1976 Hannah Tillich; Dag Hammarskjold, *Markings*, translated by W.H. Auden and Leif Sjoberg, Faber and Faber, London, and Alfred A. Knopf, New York; The Literary Trustees of Walter de la Mare and the Society of Authors as their representative for the February 29 entry by Walter de la Mare; Logan Pearsall Smith, *All Trivia*, Constable Publishers; Helen Waddell, *Beasts and Saints*, Constable Publishers; Alexander Elchaninov, *Diary of a Russian Priest*, Faber and Faber; Harold S. Kushner, *Why Bad Things Happen to Good People*, Pan Books Ltd, London, and Schocken Books, New York, published by Pantheon Books, a division of Random House Inc.; Primo Levi, *The Wrench*, the Jane Gregory Agency on behalf of Simon and Schuster; Antoine Saint Exupery, *The Little Prince* William Heinemann and Harcourt Brace Jovanovich, New York; Jean Marc Pottiez and Laurens van der Post, *A Walk with a White Bushman*, Chatto and Windus Ltd; the executors of the W.H. Davies Estate for permission to quote from *Autobiography of a Supertramp*, Jonathan Cape Ltd; Simon Weil, *Gravity and Grace*, Routledge and Kegan Paul Ltd; Erich Fromm, *The Art of Loving*, Unwin Hyman Ltd and Harper and Row, Publishers, Inc, New York.

PICTURE CREDITS

Joyce Haddon for her pictures; *Everlasting Flowers, Flowers on the Cliff, Wildflower Meadow, Poppies, A Walk in the Country, Afternoon Tea, The Armchair, The Tea Table* Fine Art Photographic Library Ltd; Hendrik Barend Koekkoek, *Figures in a Winter Landscape*; George Clausen, *Planting the Tree*; Myles Birkett Foster, *The Young Hay Gatherers*; After Miles Birkett Foster, *Gathering Primroses*; Edgar Barclay, *A Picnic in the Woods*; William Armitage, *Playing on the Beach*; William Bromley, *Gathering Blackberries*; Myles Birkett Foster, *Burnham Beeches*; Sidney Pike, *Winter Sunset* Priory Gallery: C.E. Wilson, *Girl Picking Primroses*; Kate Colls, *Girls in Flowery Meadow*.

Celia Haddon writes regularly about animals for *The Daily Telegraph*. This is the fifth of her anthologies. Others, available from Michael Joseph, are *A Christmas Posy, A Lover's Posy, A Mother's Posy* and *The Book of Friends and Friendship*. Married to author Ronald Payne, she lives half in the town and half in the country where she relaxes by growing herbs, vegetables and flowers. A rescued black and white cat, Fat Ada, completes the household.